blink again

BLINK AGAIN

sudden fiction from the upper midwest

edited by

John Colburn, Michelle Filkins & Margaret Miles

Spout Press
Minneapolis, MN

blink again
sudden fiction
from the upper midwest

ISBN 978-0-9835478-0-8

Edited by John Colburn, Michelle Filkins and Margaret Miles
Cover art by Tony Watercott
Text layout by Stefni Bell and John Colburn
cover design by

SUPERHUMAN

http://superhumanbrands.com

First Edition
Printed in the United States of America

Spout Press is a member of CLMP and is distributed to the trade by Small Press Distribution, Berkeley, CA
(www.spdbooks.org)

The story "Bomb Threat" has previously appeared in *The Rake*; the story "A Dog's Life" previously appeared in *Milwaukee Magazine*. Grateful acknowledgment is made to the editors.

Published by
Spout Press
P.O. Box 581067
Minneapolis, MN 55458-1067

I shut my eyes and all the world drops dead.
I lift my eyes and all is born again.
—Sylvia Plath

contents

alan davis
the glory of teamwork 11

andrea worth
first thing was, they shot all the dogs 17

bayard godsave
mean little seed 20

c.j. hribal
this dog's life 26

cezarija abartis
union losses 31

christopher jones
night at lick's, again 34

christy namee erickson
peace 36

cindra halm
bitter 39

danielle miller
the men 42

david bengtson
what happens? 45

dessa wander
fantastic 4 48

diane glancy
the monkey tree 53

edward micus
twice 56

ellen dworsky
shake and burn 61

emily graves
mood music 65

hannah shepard
please hold me the forgotten way 70

jarda cervenka
people's delights 73

jay orff
the mystery formations 77

jessy greene
ride to paradise 79

k.c. hanson
the gulf 84

kathryn knudson
this is what would have happened 88

kevin carollo
the glory of teamwork 91

kim teeple
go to hell, franklin 97

lon otto
a small, dark, roaring moon 104

martin brick
the thing about rain 109

maureen aitken
tainted
roby burns 115

melanie richards
first fall 126

nick healy
squirt 130

pat cumbie
hey you 136

patricia zontelli
so this is 142

patrick hueller
divorce
end zone 148

ray gonzalez
available for an epiphany 151

ronald wallace
jackknife 155

shana youngdahl
why my left leg is longer 157

sigrid tornquist
swimming lessons 163

sue taylor
bomb threat 167

sun yung shin
isolette 172

suzanne nielsen
angel's eye 177

tony rauch
how you felt when I
disappointed you 182

what we have instead of god

alan davis

"I don't need anyone to protect me," Lucy said into the telephone. A deck of tarot cards was spread across her bed. A glass of something brown was balanced between her thighs. She had on white socks, a pair of cutoffs and a tee shirt, which proclaimed that human rights have no boundaries. The card at the center of the tarot deck represented a Fool, one poised at the edge of a cliff absorbed in his own thoughts. A dog at his feet barked out a warning, but it went unheeded. He had all of his belongings in a little bag and his clothes were ragged. He carried a red rose in one hand and high above him the sun was hot and white.

In the kitchen, the phone now wedged between her chin and a shoulder, she filled a plastic bowl with blocks of tofu marinated with a chili plum paste. "That's how you see it," she said. "That's your opinion." She covered the bowl with plastic and put it in the refrigerator. "In my opinion, I'm a free woman."

At that instant the doorbell rang.

It was past midnight.

Outside the stoop was empty. The night glistened with rain and the streetlight on the corner rang in her eyes like a halo of light. The telephone was still in her hand. She could hear a tinny voice inside it call out LucyLucy Lucy. A small dog barked someplace nearby. She stared into her house as though she had rung the bell. She laid the telephone on the stoop. Then she rang the bell, twice, three times, and slipped behind a shrub. When nobody came out, she crept to a window on the east side of the house.

"Nobody home," she said.

Inside, through curtains halfway drawn, she saw the mussed bed, the half-empty bottle of booze, the deck of cards fanned out across the comforter. Solitaire, she thought. Somebody's playing solitaire. Probably an insomniac, one playing the Fool. She crept to another window, closer to the bed, and stared at the Fool, nestled between the Magician and the High Priestess. The Magician had a wand and was pointing at the earth with his other hand. He wore a slender crown around his brow. An infinity sign floated above his head. The High Priestess sat in a temple between two columns, one light and one dark, with a sacred roll in her lap. A veil waved in the wind above her.

A crescent moon lay under her left foot.

Lucy crept on all fours, like Orpheus in the underworld, from window to window. She climbed a chain link fence out back and peered into the bath, where a bar of French milled soap glistened green in a silver dish by the tub. A sock monkey hung by one furry arm from the underside of the dish.

Ding dong ditch. Ding dong ditch. That was it, a game played as a kid, one of those things that had something to do with puberty. *Ring the bell, run like hell.* She could still remember the chant. She had been the ringleader, wore a green kerchief to hide her face, buzzed or knocked with glee on a dozen doors a night even after the adults on her block made a kind of vigilante group to stop it. They would never catch her. Never in hell.

Ding dong ditch. That was it. What a hoot, like Mark Twain in San Francisco throwing rocks on tin roofs to disturb people's sleep and make a racket.

She had recovered from a long, deep illness but had never recovered that youthful happiness. That was what she had lost. Ding dong ditch.

It was time again to disturb people's sleep, to make a racket.

She circled the house, peered into each window, and then came back to the stoop, where the phone waited. As if on cue, it started ringing like a cry from some other more angelic world. Before she picked it up, she noticed that there was a crescent moon in the night sky and that an emerald green star blinked high above her like a doorbell just waiting to be buzzed.

It was time and past time to go, to bang on the world and make it glow like struck prongs on a tuning fork. Give it all up and run. The phone would be her wand. She waved it above her head. She could hear tinny voices shout out her name. LucyLucyLucy.

"Not me Not me Not me," she shouted at the sky. The small dog still barked its warning. *Life is what happens while you're busy making other plans,* it was singing. If I have to play the Fool, she thought, better do it with open eyes. She flung open her front door, reached inside to grab a small red bag that fit on her shoulders like a backpack. She scrambled through the house and filled it. The sock monkey, the French milled soap.

Outside again, she rang her doorbell twice, yelled "Ding Dong Ditch Ding Dong Ditch."

A group of kids in big floppy pants with cargo pockets and baseball caps turned back on their heads sneaked like commandos on a concrete porch, rang a bell and skedaddled like slapstick cartoons. When she ran past the house, the door opened and a heavyset grizzled man with a plaid shirt glared at her.

"I saw you!" he shouted. "I called the cops. We'll get you. We'll get you, goddammit. You won't be free for long."

Not for long, not for long, but long enough to play the Fool.

It was the end of her regular life. This was a new one.

Not for long. She hummed with words under her breath. "You've got to catch me first," she shouted to the crescent moon.

She smiled into the moisture of the night and ran hard in her white socks.

Sweat glistened on her forehead. It felt good. Her only belongings bounced in the bag on her back. It felt good, running to the naked world with its crescent moon and green star.

She sang "Happy Woman Blues."

She was no longer Lucy. She was a singer of little songs, Fool, Magician, High Priestess. She proved that night and every night as she ran for her life from town to town that she could read the world like a pack of cards. She became an urban legend, ringing doorbells, getting her food and love on the run while men and women trapped in their lives heard the bells ring late at night and imagined a new, naked world. If someone fast on his feet surprised her, by luck or sleight of hand, she gave a big bug-eyed stare, turned quickly in her socks, waved her telephone into the sky, and shouted MeMeMe, so happy that the muscles in her face were bound to break.

first thing was, they shot all the dogs

andrea worth

Both his doors were kicked in at the same time. Men with sharp elbows. Guns drawn. Quick dead-on shots to the scruff mutts and the fat, meat legged bulldogs. *Get them up. Get those fucking hands up.* Some of the men had walkie-talkies. Least that's what he'd called them when he got a pair as a kid – he'd taken the things apart, couldn't get them back together right. Dark hacked plastic pieces and wires. Dead air. Nothing he had ever lasted long.

They cuffed his wrists while his arms were raised. Padded him down. Then turned over all the drawers, dumped the dog food containers. Uncovered the duffel sacks, stuffed like body bags. Ninety pounds of dope. One of the dogs whined. Only half dead. Wind howled through the gaping doorways, pushed out the yeasted smell of the morning's beer. Sun sliced between the blinds, reflecting suspended specks of dust and ash. They knew enough to pull out hacksaws and cut along the walls, where they found stacks of cash between the sheetrock and the studs.

He closed his eyes, remembered back ten years: junior high, sitting on the bus, behind Faith. Prettiest girl he knew. *Gimme your book.* He opened it, drew a big-boobed woman leaning over the head of a dead president. Faith laughed. Beside him, his buddies, a fat one without front teeth and a skinny one who'd had his hands on every good girl in school, flung spitballs through straws. When the bus driver said *Enough,* one of them yelled *Fuck you fat shit* and they were three all out the door. Outside. High-tops slipping in the snow. Breath iced white. So what? He had a couple fatties he'd bought off the pig farmer. Three bucks a joint, four for weed laced with PCP. It was something to do. He winked at Faith through a brown screen of exhaust as the bus lurched away. Then he and his buddies lay down on the frosted back road and smoked. He held smoke heat in his lungs until he couldn't feel the cold seep through his jean jacket. He thought it could always be like this: high bright sky, puffs of clouds that rolled as if the world was greased. Easy.

He opened his eyes. Knew what was coming. Possession. Distribution. Federal offenses for crossing state lines. And he'd crossed every line he could. On the floor, one of the dogs twitched. A final movement in the spreading puddle of drool and piss and blood. Just a dumb mutt that never tried to hurt anybody. He wanted to put his hands on that dog one more time, before he was gone cold. He moved forward out of instinct. They shoved him back, *Keep your fucking hands up and don't move.* He reached into the empty air. His arms ached as if the sky was pressing down. As if it was made of dead weight.

mean little seed

bayard godsave

"Tell us a story, Jones."

His face orange and grooved in the light of the watch-fire, Jones spat into the darkness. "I ever tell you about the time I seen them put the Pope on trial?"

He had. But the men said nothing.

Jones spat once more. "I saw the Pope alive only once," he said, "in front of the theater on a Sunday afternoon, where all the men were out smoking, taking in the air and talking as men do on Sundays at intermission. His face was narrow and hard like an antelope's skull, and his mouth a confusion of knuckly teeth, not unlike the Slav's. I've heard it told that, as a young man, the Pope used the severed head of an enemy for a football. Of course, I've heard similar tales told of the indigenous tribes who'd once lived in the woods around that town—I've heard a great deal of the historic indigenous atrocities attributed at one time or another to the Pope. But wherever the truth lies in the details of such claims, the Pope's cruelty was never in doubt; you could see it in how he stood apart from other men, in the flatness of his gaze. And I could see it that day, out in front of the theater as his subordinates flapped and chattered about him, and him only staring past them, their insignificance turning them already to shades, to phantom specters before him.

"It was one of those very subordinates, a tall and fisheyed Swede named Pedersen who filled the empty shoes of the Pope upon his passing—a natural enough death, they said, a blood vessel rupturing at the base of his brain while he slept—and it was the Swede Pedersen that announced the Pope's being charged with the crime of conspiracy, conspiracy to corrupt the moral and spiritual uprightness of the township and her citizens. 'The very citizens he swore an oath to protect,' Pedersen said from the courthouse steps on the third day after the Pope's body had been surrendered back to the earth."

Some of the men had run steel cables above the watch-fire and had draped salted sheets of horsemeat over them. The cables sang and whined in the heat and the horse-flesh whistled and popped as small globes of fat dropped from it and evaporated in the fire.

"So Pedersen ordered the Pope's body exhumed and brought to the courthouse," Jones said.

"His clothes were dusty, as though they'd been shut up in an attic for too long. His eyes, which remained open and unblinking for the length of his trial, were dried-out and beginning to wrinkle. And as the days progressed the Pope's skin took on a grayish cast and started flaking away in places.

"Pedersen called on witness after witness to testify to the Pope's offenses. One spoke of the Pope's men fouling his well-water with rotting livestock after he'd denied the Pope logging rights to his land. Another told of the Pope's carving off a valet's nose over the sum of a livery bill. But it was the proceedings of the second afternoon that eclipse for strangeness anything I'd seen before and most of what I've seen since.

"Pedersen, the Swede, when the court returned from lunch that day, called the Pope himself to the stand.

"Three of Pedersen's deputies were charged with physically moving the Pope. By this time, of course, his body was set with rigor and stiff as a store-window display. A ripple of laughter passed through the gallery as the deputies tipped the seated corpse on its side and carried it like an armchair and positioned it next to the judge's bench. Pedersen rose and stood in silence in front of the corpse for a moment before opening with his first question.

"'How do you respond, sir,' he said, 'to the charges this court has brought against you?'

"The Pope's countenance remained unchanged. All of us there in the gallery looked on, unable to convince ourselves fully that Pedersen was pursuing this particular line of madness, but at the same time wanting desperately to see him follow it all the way.

"Pedersen paced back and forth across the width of the courtroom, the floorboards creaking and banging under his nervous footfalls. He stopped and stood in front of the Pope. 'What do you have to say to these people before you, sir,' he said, sweeping his arm slowly in our direction, 'who have lived in fear of you for so long? Whose lives have each been so maliciously touched by your wickedness?'

"Pedersen continued in this fashion for some time, his arms flailing ever wilder as he berated the tyrant's cast-off vessel, its eyes staring out unseeing past the hot-tempered Swede even as they did in life.

"Well, Pedersen whipped himself up into such a state that he failed to notice entirely when the corpse began to stir ever so faintly in the dock, as though the Pope's spirit had once again animated its flesh and was preparing to put his one-time subordinate back in his place."

Jones paused here, fished a cigarette from his shirt

pocket and lit it before going on. "But those of us there in the gallery that day saw it," he said. "And Pedersen must have noticed that some change had come over us, because he soon fell into silence and turned to face the Pope. The corpse wobbled a bit in its seat, its head began to tremble, as if with rage, then all at once its jaw dropped open with a short tearing sound, as might accompany your pulling a drumstick free from a cooked duck. We sat still and waited, held our collective breath, and half expected the Pope to speak. But the corpse just sat there, its mouth agape, showing us its tongue, brown and hard like a hank of jerky."

A wind picked up and blew across the watch-fire, embers dancing and tumbling along it out into the dark. Jones, it seemed, was not going to continue, this part of his story being as good a place as any to stop. "And Pedersen? The Swede?" one of the men said. "Whatever became of him?"

"The Swede," Jones said, "in time became himself a tyrant. And later, I'm told, was stoned to death by the citizens of that town for reasons I don't know. Such is the way of things in this world. The weak grow increasingly less fearful under tyranny until one day their tyrant is cast down. But the weak too grow forgetful and themselves become tyrants only to find that they are one day cast down and so on."

The men stared thoughtfully into the fire. In the coming days half of them would die, and many more would be afflicted with hobblings and deformities, with blindness and insanity. They were the weak, they knew this much, but whether they were the weak grown less fearful, or the weak grown forgetful, was harder for them to say. In the end, they would all agree, whichever it was they were didn't matter very much at all. Not when you really thought about it.

this dog's life

c.j. hribal

1.

The dog follows its nose. At Nessun Dorma and Onopa people dining outside sometimes feed it directly from their tables. And if not, there are always the bins out back. It remembers the leash, remembers the yank back when it found an enticing chicken bone. It can eat things now the man used to yell at it for even sniffing. The girl, too—"No," she'd yell, "No! No!" as though loving what made you sick was a crime. It eats its fill now.

2.

They are at the Oriental Theater. Buddhas line the walls, red teardrops of serenity in their foreheads. The Wurlitzer—imagine a theater with a still-functioning Wurlitzer!—swirls happily. Applause, applause; the Wurlitzer man waves and keeps playing as he disappears into the floor. Jules, fifteen, has never been here before.

Her new friends—Amy and Arthur—are cool in ways Jules is not. They ask her, "What did you.get?"

"iPod mini, cell phone, a couple of credit cards, fifteen bucks. You?"

Amy speaks for herself and Arthur. "Two Blackberries, a Thinkpad, a couple of cells, a checkbook, half a dozen credit cards and a hundred and eighty bucks. You grabbed a backpack, didn't you? We went after the suits."

"I figured if I was caught I could say I grabbed it by mistake."

"Dare to be great," says Arthur, like he is holding her to a higher standard.

"I miss my mom," says Jules, who is tired of shuttling between her mom's place and her father's. She's supposedly staying with her mother this week. Her mother is in Florida with her boyfriend getting tan.

"And how IS your mom?"

Jules slugs him.

"I was only asking."

"Don't ask."

3.

The dog remembers trotting with the man on a serpentine parkway, bikes and cars and families picnicking.

There was an abandoned pool in the park's middle, a golf course, a river. That was a while ago. The dog is shuttled now between a duplex on Vliet Street near the tonier Highlands and a duplex off Humboldt and Center in Riverwest. The girl, too.

4.

The woman has given up on walking the dog. The man as well. They let him out, let him wander the streets in their new, respective neighborhoods. They would ask the girl to walk him, but the girl disappears with her new friends right after school. "I have better things to do!" she screams. That is what the man told the woman a couple years ago. The woman was relieved the man said it first. It absolved her of saying it herself.

5.

The dog likes its new life. It hears its name, dimly, each day, from farther and farther away. So many things to sniff, so many treats to find. People pat its head, stroke its flanks. They say things like, "Are you my baby? Are you my good girl?"

It's nice. Still, the dog remembers its old life. It thinks, not really sure about this, that maybe something was lost, and is anxious about this. What was lost? What, what?

6.

"I miss my dog." Jules is with Arthur at a midnight showing of *The Rocky Horror Picture Show*. She feels grown-up and weird in her torn fishnet stockings and push-up bra and maid's uniform. Amy's somewhere else. She and Arthur had a fight about something.

Halfway through the movie Arthur is holding her hand. "I thought the dog went with you from your mom's house to your dad's."

"It does, but he ran away. Dad says he's lost. My mom says she never liked that dog anyway, it was mostly my dad's dog in the first place, and good riddance to both of them."

"Harsh."

"She's working on putting distance between our old life and her new one."

"You should, too." Which is when Arthur kisses her and puts his hand inside her bra. Later Arthur takes her to the river, to the old stone bridge where couples go who do this sort of thing. They leave the car because it's a warm night and after some fumbling Jules finds herself looking at the stars while Arthur pants himself into a frenzy on top of her. She has seen dogs doing this, and though the arrangement was different, she bets the feeling is the same—one dog moves with blind, desperate fury, and the other accepts this with forlorn patience. When Arthur is finished quivering on top of her she says, "I miss my dog," and Arthur has a hard time getting her to stop crying.

7.

Eventually the dog finds its way home again. He'd been fed by a nice older woman who'd kept him at her house, but after a few days he found a low spot under her fence and dug his way free. He needed to be somewhere—of that he was certain. When he gets home—it's the man's home, he can tell by the shape and the smell of the bushes surrounding the stoop—everyone is happy to see him. "The prodigal son returns," says the man. The girl cries into his neck. Something about her smells different. He licks her cheek anyway, thumps his tail—the dog equivalent of a shrug—as she strokes his back and strokes his skull between his ears.

Dogs are used to disappointment.

union losses

cezarija abartis

Ruth helped the old woman with her baggage. Ruth was not so young herself, forty-three. She regarded the old woman with distaste—why such a heavy suitcase for only one week?

The woman introduced herself as Naomi. "What a coincidence—I mean, our names come from the Bible."

Ruth made a small smile in acknowledgment, and carried Naomi's linens and suitcase to a downstairs room. They had arrived in Port Townsend on the same shuttle for the writers' workshops. This was the beautiful edge of the continent; she hoped she would not fall off. Naomi said it was her anniversary, but she was a widow. "On our thirty-fifth wedding anniversary, I made a toast to George, 'To the second thirty-five years.' He answered back, 'And to the third. And the fourth.' Funny man."

Back in her own room, Ruth shut her window. She sat at the desk and arranged on it her clock, pens, paper.

One of the ballpoint pens was out of ink. She tossed it into the brown metal trash can; it made a clanging sound. For their anniversary four years ago, Brian had given her a Montblanc with a pearly barrel. Last year, of course, there was nothing.

Ruth paced in the room. When she passed the mirror, she screwed her face up and made a net of wrinkles like Naomi's; she did not recognize herself. She heard a knock on the door. She opened it; Naomi extended a paper bag. "I packed a bag of cookies at home." Her white hair seemed soft around her face, holy.

"I bake cookies now." Naomi shrugged. "Before I retired, I used to be a union organizer for the typographers."

Ruth invited her to sit down. A retired union organizer. She wryly thought of the dissolution of her own union. There had been a time when Brian enjoyed her wryness.

Ruth placed the brown paper bag on her desk next to the alarm clock. Outside the window, the red sun rolled on the bay, spreading the water flat beneath two sailboats that glinted on the horizon. She turned toward Naomi. She had not flicked on the overhead light, and they were both brushed with damp twilight.

Naomi said that union membership had gone down

from more than twenty per cent of the work force to twelve.

Ruth said that unions were not doing well since Reagan crushed the air traffic controllers. That was the easy and agreeable thing to say. "Wasn't that the case?"

Sitting on the edge of the bed, Naomi looked down and nodded, holding herself in, as if there were an abyss she could fall into.

Ruth saw Naomi's unease, or perhaps it was she herself who was rattled and unmoored. Outside, the world was pulsing, shimmering. Ruth felt her own heart beating in rhythm with the wobbling planet.

She sat beside Naomi and held on to the bed. "Will it get better? I mean, eventually, later—at some later time? Do you have hope?"

"Of course," Naomi said. She looked up, and her eyes invited the world in.

night at lick's, again

christopher jones

Gertie Black-Knacker, the faded and overripe petunia of Lick's Liquor Shanty, raised her loose-skinned hand to signal for another round. The bartender, Guano Pete, said "One foot in the coffin, Gert?"

"Is that all, Pete? Feels like 'em both." This was their little joke, the name of her drink-of-necessity, One Foot in the Coffin, shot of rail whiskey, half-and-half back. Gertie needed something demanding to pursue the house whiskey, a tender treat called Sassy Cracker's Armpit Mash, so pestilent a brew that the poison wept through the bottle's glass to char the label. She was a wreck, but not that wrecked.

Thumps and screams erupted from the ceiling and a burning gob flamed down into the parking lot outside. Old Sonny Nerd was up there again, every night he'd get all revved up on Mongoose Gin, steal all the flammables from the men's room and clamber arthritically onto the steep-pitched roof of the bar to claim it for Spain and defend against all comers. Every night, Sonny stamping and shrieking, the parking lot a no-man's-land obstacle course as stilted Hell rained down flaming rolls of toilet paper, burning towels, loose slates, and finally, the old gin-soaked rummy himself, crashing to earth with the saltine crunch of bone.

Pete set the glasses down in front of Gertie's place at the bar. She moved them around each other like a mutual orbit, a little dance to the Tourette's cadence Sonny beat on the roof. She drank them down slowly, lingering over both the hot hurt of the mash and the cloying relief of the cream, its cataract white a theory of clean none of them could remember.

Guano inclined his head toward the exhausted possibilities of her glasses, raised and eyebrow of inquiry to Gertie.

"I don't know, Pete, I think I've had enough."

"Yeah, haven't we all, Gertie. So, was that a Yes?"

"Yeah, I suppose it was. Both feet this time, huh? What else we gonna do?"

peace

christy namee erickson

Here's my theory on peace. If I loved everyone and everyone loved me then I think that'd be pretty peaceful but it'd also have to be pretty perfect and pretty forgiving and I'm just not so sure it's all like that. If I wake up in the morning and I think, love your neighbor! I could do that but that lets my neighbor off the hook for a lot of shit she pulls. I think people who love peace are those asshole neighbors that everyone's nice to anyway so it's not like they gotta work at it. If anyone's peaceful, it's me, putting up with their peacenik asses. I wouldn't be caught dead doing the peace thing, not on this planet, not in this body anyway.

My neighbor is out walking late. I don't see her, but Francisco does. He points her out to me, after she passed the car and he looked up from my lips, his loved leaned up against me in the passenger seat.

"Shit," I say. "You better go now." This confuses him,

as it should. We're having a good time.

He kisses me again, then again, then again.

"No really," I stammer, between breaths, between thoughts. "We can't be doing this here."

"Why not?" he asks, in that voice, the one that's not really a question.

I pause, looking him over, lost in all his dark features, heart in my fingertips, sparks against our yellow and cinnamon skins like flames.

"You see those houses?" I say. He nods. He sees the houses. "All white. I haven't seen that neighbor since she called the police on me. "

"Seriously?" he's temporarily paying attention.

"For real. My roommate has a party with a bunch of white people, no police. I have a party, everybody freaks out and calls the cops. I even told her I was having the people over and she said that sounded great. Fucker."

"Yah, I don't like them gringo girls," he agrees. He's tracing my face with his nose.

"I'm for real. She can't be seeing me like this. I gotta go to court now cos of her."

"For real? Mammita, you gotta go to court?" He smiles. *Grand sonreisa,* all up in my anger.

I giggle but purse my lips, trying to take it back. "You see what I'm sayin?" I ask, my eyes swirling up at him. I massage the back of his head, my fingers entwined with his black waves, and I draw a line around his soft jaw, a thumb petting the small patch of hair on his chin.

"I could drive around the corner," he suggests.

"Franciso."

"I'm just sayin."

"I'm just sayin."

"I'm just—"

"Shhh," I look up at the house, thinking I saw a light come on. It's a big house, an old one, that's what Francisco had said. A sweet Christmas wreath hung on my neighbor's door, colorful Tibetan peace flags bannered across the entryway. I look at my door, bare, a wrinkly morning glory vine I planted last summer frozen and flaccid nearby. A two-foot smiling ceramic pumpkin man with overalls stands between them, still leftover from Halloween.

I gather my things, wrapping a scarf around my neck an extra time. "They're all the same, boo. You know they're all the same."

bitter

cindra halm

After the radiation treatments, my mother wanted only green bananas. Bananas that weren't even fruit yet, not a drop of sweetness throughout.

"These I can taste," she said. "My tongue has all but died."

She hadn't died. Yet. Although she was past bargaining with God, she still wanted to barter with me. She would try to quit smoking, she said, but only if I promised not to drink and drive.

"Ah…you must be thinking of one of your children from a previous life. Mom, it's me, Charlene, remember—the nerd? I barely drink, and I don't even own a car."

Tears appeared as spontaneously as an accident. The past hung tenaciously onto her eyelash like an unripe fruit. I caught a glimpse of my younger, glamorous mother, dazzled and bewildered, plucked from circumstances and asked to dance.

"One has regrets." She stared. "And requests."

"Ok; it's a deal," I said.

Soon, the materiality of the bananas grew indigestible. The disease or the treatment had turned her stomach, so she switched to chocolate, the darker the better. Less solid, still strong. She could taste it along the back of her life, she said.

She got the idea from *To Kill a Mockingbird*. She wouldn't smoke while I read aloud, two whole hours. Instead, she ate one square of 85% cocoa bit by oily crumb. Like scary Mrs. Dubose, she'd drool, curse, and shake until the timer sounded. Unlike Jem, I hadn't been made to read to her as apology for my temper. Still, guilt tapped my shoulder like an addict.

I lied to keep my bargain. After readings, my mother's back was straight as a dancer's as she bragged of her twitchy muscles, dry mind, wavy mouth. She'd had two fewer cigarettes than the day before. I said I was trying, but that the cravings were too strong; I couldn't resist always having one more beer. Worse, I'd crashed into the garage door, mangled it and the fender too.

"An accident means you didn't mean it." She spat from the back of her tongue. "Bastard. I didn't mean it."

By the time I was bringing her Turkish coffee for her meals, my mother's words were turning to steam. Still, she put her hand on mine when I relayed my troubles.

"Mom, I'm so sorry. Last night, Mom, I hit a cat. I killed it; horrible, Mom. I promise I'll stop now; I really will."

"Relapse...cat..." she whispered. "Reprieve..."

As always, books were closed, stories told and not told. I wanted to sit on the aqua couch at the coffee shop and stare at the mural of Audrey Hepburn; I wanted to hear Jem's father in the book say, "She was the bravest person I ever knew." Shifting in the café line from foot to foot, I'm not sure what I forgave my mother for.

Maybe the smell of the roasting beans would be enough to open the cliffhanger back of my throat. Myself, I'd never had a cup of joe; I was thinking of trying one, that universal morning bitter. In front of me, the black liquid poured.

the men

danielle miller

The men are standing in their garage, breathing midwinter air and huffing cigars. The yard of the house is snow gray, the streets murky black from car oil and exhaust. One two three quick drags on their cigars before they blow the smoke into each other's faces. Four chickadees hop from branch to branch in a small bare tree. The wife is inside, drinking quietly on the couch and wondering if she should pretend to cry. The two men, the two brothers, sit and stand in the half lit garage watching the cold air crawl in through the open garage door.

"Screw you."

"Yeah, screw you."

The men are angry and blowing smoke, letting the cold air burn their noses and the backs of their throats. The men have a lot to say because their mother died. A car crunches by on the road, scaring the birds. The mother froze to death in her little house because she couldn't pay for heating and the furnace shut off in the night. The older brother is chilled in his canvas jacket and tries to feel dying. The lamppost down the street turns on, then off. The men throw the ends of their cigars on the ground one after another and watch them roll on the smooth cement, still smoking. Someone opens up the rest of the cigar package. The thin plastic crunches and the gold foil is broken. Everything smells like old cardboard and tobacco. The wife sips around the lip of the bottle. She can't taste the alcohol anymore, but her eyes water. The two men, the two brothers, look each other in the eyes, still, one two three blow.

"I hate this."

"Shut up."

The men close their eyes and lean back. The wife decides to take her shirt off. The brothers are thinking about their rotting guts and there's a lot to say since one of them has always been older. The younger shifts his weight and knocks the kerosene off a shelf. The can opens all over his pants and he lets the cigar slip from between his lips. A squirrel weaves through the naked branches of the bush across the street. The mother is buried forty miles away, there's no snow there. The cigar hits the man's pants and the fire jumps out quick in the cold air. The man lets it burn for a moment, shocked, before he smothers the fire against his other leg. The older brother is unsatisfied and angry. He presses the red end of his cigar against the other man's pants. Fire jumps again. The wife is looking for change in the couch cushions, she took her bra off. The older man wants his brother to fall, to be consumed, but somehow the fire goes out. The younger brother is panting, his leg black. An orange cat rushes across the road and icy lawns. The pants are lit again and the burning man falls onto the cement, rolling in greasy puddles and screaming. The mother always wore a brown shawl and slippers. In the coffin she wore white. The wind rattles and everything smells charred. The man stops the flames but his skin is still burning. The older brother is angry. He would have liked to sweep the ashes out into the snow.

what happens?

david bengtson

Not words of kindness, that's not the problem. But words of anger, disappointment, confrontational words. What happens when these words are packed away in cardboard boxes and stacked in the attic? Are sent to the basement and lined up against a wall like storm windows in summer?

A man who loves flowers has placed in every space in his house pots of all sizes filled with rich soil. He has planted seeds, at just the right depth. Watered and fertilized and rotated them so that each pot is bathed in sunlight for at least part of every day.

Most every seed germinates and pushes its little head through the soil, grows and grows. Until the house is filled with the fresh scent of opening buds. Until the house is alive with flowers of every shape and color.

When the man falls into sleep, he dreams of a large eye that stares at him, occasionally blinks, slowly, deliberately. One night, when the eyelid opens, he thinks he sees a man walking away, across a fallow field, with a flower pot in each outstretched hand, looking like a T, maybe even a cross.

This dream scares the man, and the next morning he begins to carry the flower pots, two at a time, from the house to the pile of rocks on the other side of the field, his arms outstretched, a pot in each hand. He does this until all of the pots have been removed. He sets them on the rocks, sometimes balancing them precariously.

After the last pots have been set in place, he turns his back to them and begins to walk home. Halfway across the field, he remembers the story of Lot and his wife and wonders what will happen if he looks back. He turns his head slowly. Over his right shoulder he sees the sun setting behind the flowers, their colors now turning to shadow as the night sky lowers.

Back at home he walks from room to empty room, pulls each of the window shades tight to the sill. Now what will he do? He knows he can't go back to the flowers. They will live or die without him. He sits at the kitchen table, carefully gathers the scattered grains of soil into a small pile in front of him. He is afraid to close his eyes.

He walks down the stairs to the basement, bends, picks up the first thing he sees, a tiny clay pot, somehow left behind. Before he realizes what he is doing, he throws it with all his might, then listens, as every pane of glass shatters, almost simultaneously.

fantastic 4

dessa wander

It started when I was on hold—an unusual moment for beginnings. A pair of automated voices was keeping me informed of my cue position. "You are caller number *TWO*. There are *ONE* callers ahead of you." The primary voice was soothing and erotic, the other robotic, specializing in numbers exclusively. I had a little daydream about a call center populated by only centerfolds and fembots--the former wrapping spiral cords around their fingers, taking calls in negligee, the latter sitting erect, reciting numbers into their headsets, and blinking in unison, with a shutter click. A real receptionist abruptly cut in, "Hello, thank you for holding. May I ask who's calling?" Disoriented by the sudden bombardment of different female voices, I answered, "Fantastic."

The receptionist, surprised by my answer, repeated, "Fantastic?"

"Yes. Fantastic."

Please remember that this entire exchange transpired in the course of two or three seconds. And I have relived these few moments many times, slowing down the reel of my memory to determine exactly what went wrong. Here's the frame-by-frame analysis: I'd been lulled into a semi-stupor by long minutes on hold. When the receptionist jarred me back to attention, I answered the question that usually begins a social conversation: *How are you?* When the receptionist sought to confirm that she'd heard me correctly, I kneejerked a literal answer: *Yes. The word I just said was the word 'Fantastic.'* Had I been allowed even another fraction of a second, I would have bailed myself out with some quick, banal explanation. "But my name is Alicia Olson—forgive me, haven't had my coffee yet." We would each produce a puff of laughter and she'd reciprocate with some corporate quip—Hump Day or what have you—and the entire fumble would be corrected. But I was too slow.

"Alright Fantastic, I'll patch you through."

Then I was holding again. But this hold was different. Dark. Empty. I was not, of course, making a social call. I had called *Harper's Magazine* about a job—an editorial position vacated only the week before. I moved to hang up, but hesitated for a moment at the thought that *Harper's* might have Caller ID. Too slow.

"Good morning Fantastic, this is Ellen Rosenbush. I understand you're calling about our Arts Editor position?"

Ellen and I stayed on the line for thirty-five minutes. I've never had a better interview. We're both passionate Lorca fans. We both think Chicago's overrated, much more like Gotham than New York is. We both hate the word 'paradox,' which is used in practice to mean 'confusing' by a speaker who seeks to justify his confusion by deeming the issue at hand is fundamentally impossible to understand. It was one of the best phone calls I've had. It was a romantic-comedy, talk-until-the-sun-comes-up, buy-a-plane-ticket-in-the-morning sort of phone call.

At the end of our conversation, the inevitable question came, "Well Fantastic, it's really been a pleasure talking. I'm sure you must field the question all the time, but can I ask how you how you got your name?"

"My mom is from the Yucatán." As if across the border, people are naming their children book reviews.

"Ah, and what does it mean?"

"It...means... Cherished."

"*Ohhhh.* How beautiful." Ellen said this with a tone of great understanding—a tone you'd use after someone paused the movie to tell you why the guy in the grey suit was significant. I'm not sure why this explanation was so satisfying to her, since 'fantastic' means something pretty close to 'cherished' in English.

My mom is, actually, from the Yucatán. She's also a public relations consultant with a pretty high-profile client list. I felt sure that in one fell swoop I'd trespassed against both my real mom—who was busy coaching powerful executives not to fidget while issuing difficult statements—and my new, pretend mom—so profoundly smitten with American culture so as to name her children almost indiscriminately from a vocabulary she'd breathlessly lifted from infomercials.

Ellen offered me the job. I took it.

On Monday morning I reported to the office early. I met my coworkers as they filed in, drinking strong coffees in a sunlit central studio. Mandy, herself a recent hire, volunteered to provide a dime-tour. She had blunt-cut bangs and a nicotine patch and an easy laugh, and she talked and gestured with a pen in her right hand that she would ash absentmindedly every so often. We were friends by the time she showed me how to work the copy machine in the break room. The tour ended at my desk, where someone had pitched a little paper name card. Fantastic Olson: Arts Editor.

The rest of the day acquired a slow-motion quality. The phones rang from far away. Lunch was one of the most flavorful meals I had ever eaten. And I knew why: It was my last meal as the Arts Editor of *Harper's Magazine*. At the end of the day I would have to report to HR and present some ID. I set into the final hours of my dream job with the joie de vivre of the nearly dead—the smell of toner, of electricity, of Mandy's afternoon cigarette and the perfume she'd used to conceal it, all indelible. At three, I pushed aside the employee handbook and traced my finger along the whorls in the cherry wood of my desk. How wonderful, I thought, to put cowlicks in trees. To spin a whirlpool into wood. And how wonderful to find the same design at the end of each of my fingertips—ten perfect, tiny hurricanes. Each uniquely identifiable as mine. I wiped my fingerprints off the wood. I would, I decided, allow myself to simmer in one more hour of my dream job. Then I would march into her office and tell the simple truth. Ellen, I am not Fantastic. I would not stutter, I would not fidget. I would thank her for the time at the magazine, tell her I cherished every moment, and resign.

the monkey tree

diane glancy

No lions or tigers, no mamma snake, just
watermelon and the buckwheat cake. You don't
have to run through the jungle and scuff up
your feet. You be happy as a monkey in a
monkey tree.

Sonny and Brownie,
Sail Away—

Imagine a world upsidedown— the p is a b, and
the b, a p—

Sboon, fork, blate. That was what was on the taple. They said I had disblexia. Words to me were runners. They looked different to me than they did to others. I read what was on the bage but it was not what others saw. I could not understand what they saw. I could not understand why they didn't see what I saw. I wrote what I saw and they said it was not what was there. Or what was there I didn't see.

I was dubed. I was scalded. I was given eyes that did not see things the way they were seen. I came from Toma to the Willatoona school. I could not read. I could not write. The radiator was plasting. It was cold and stormy as the night Puddy Holly went down near Clear Lake just off I-35 south of the Minnesota/Iowa porder.

My father liked Sonny Terry and Prownie McGhee. He listened to their plues. Sail away with me— We will cross the mighty ocean into Charleston Pay. It was not the Atlantic coast put the packwaters of rural America where the sun never hit with its lightness. I wrote a crude sign on a biece of cardpoard and but it on my door: Charleston Pay. That's what I named my blace. I had not crossed the ocean like them, put had peen here since the peginning.

I was in school after school. None tuned out anything other than failure. The albhapet was ubsidedown. On its side. Scattered. It changed blaces pefore my eyes. Crashed. The way I sbilled a buzzle to the floor and some of the bieces lay face down and the buzzle would never go together pecause my buzzle pox didn't have a bicture of what the bieces looked like when they were together. I stood with my packback in the barking lot. Waiting for my father. I imagine butting avacados/mangos on the monkey tree. Showing them bieces of my world. Sometimes in reading, I see Puddy's face at his blane window glittering with ice that will bull him down.

What of these words loaded on a blane too heavy with cold? What of the window that sees what? The ground coming up?

The storm of misread words licks the blane. I see ice dancing as it panks into the edge of a storm tearing off my wings and I fly into this new, this bromised world.

twice

edward micus

Already the mid-morning heat was leaning on him. Not a stitch of wind, the grove hushed in shadow, crowded with heat, and the sky a cataract. To the west, one thin cloud, the color of bone, skated the horizon, and two crows rowed upward against the glare. Bracing himself against the axe as if it were a cane, he wiped his brow with a bandanna. He had felled the pine, the straightest of the six, dragged it from the treeline. He would trim and strip the bark, hew the trunk for the planks, rough plane them, and fashion a bier from the rough cuts. He would make the two coffins the same, as best he could. They had come into the world that way.

"Would be fittin'," he shouted across the grove to her, "for you to have a hand in this. Before the boys go bad."

She was rocking on the front porch, the glass of whiskey in her hand. "I'll have none of it," is what she told him.

The twins were almost four when she helped them

plant the string of pine. After they'd dug the holes and set the saplings in, each not much taller than the boys themselves, they all knelt to tamp the earth with their hands. The two went with their little pails to the pump but one tripped on a tree root on his way back, spilling his water. The other gave his brother his own pail, took the empty back to the pump for refilling, she remembered that.

She lifted her voice. "Be more fittin'," she said, "if they'd a both gone off homesteadin'. You're the one kept 'em on here."

He looked past her, through the window to the south field, freshly picked, the bones of stalks littering the field. He would plow them under in the fall, plant again in spring. Alone.

The evening before he'd asked her to drive the eighteen miles to Putney, but she refused. He hitched the buckboard to Ole' Bill, went alone to the general store.

"Terrible loss," the owner said.

"I'll need ice. Twelve penny nails."

"I'll throw the nails in."

"A bolt of cotton. Black?"

"I have blue. And I'll send out riders."

"I'm beholdin'." He looked to his hands. "Monday then, I would say. Toward evening."

They loaded the ice blocks on the wagon, threw the

sawdust on top, then a tarp. He made the trip to the homeplace at full trot. Even Ole' Bill sensed the urgency.

When he entered the root cellar, he thought to find the boys washed and laid out, but that was not to be. He did it himself, wrestling the two into the Sunday shirts and trousers they had outgrown, but he managed it. He cut two squares from a scrap of cardboard and wrote in his best script, 'Henry' then 'Harvey' and pinned the names on the lapels. He covered the ice blocks, which were gritty with sawdust, with a bedsheet, hoisted the two on top, covered them again with another sheet, a hunk of burlap around that, and the tarp, tucking it in as best he could beneath the iceblock, and went back into the house.

He found her in the parlor rocking, a whiskey still in her hand. After he made his own supper, he walked past her toward the stairway. "Are you all right?" he asked her. She would not look at him. "It's tired me out, all of it," he said, and climbed the stairs.

She was already in the parlor rocking, her coffee on the daystand, the whiskey beside it, when he came down in the morning. He saw the names of the boys he had written on the cardboard scraps rocking in her lap. She had gotten up in the night with a lantern, stumbled somehow to the cellar, undid the pile, took the names away.

"Did you cover them?" he asked her.

"They'll be no showin', no viewin'," she told him. She looked down to the names in her lap. "I know the difference. Do you?"

He went to the shed to finish what had to be done. Midafternoon his neighbor to the west arrived with a kettle of stew and two jugs of rum, his box of tools. They finished the second box, fashioned the biers from scrap.

"I thought to put the two in one box. Have you heard of it?"

"No," the neighbor said.

They brought the biers to the parlor, settled them against the north wall, then covered them with the blue cloth. They finished and took the coffins to the cellar, unwrapped the two boys and hoisted them in. He nailed down the lid. "She'd have it this way," he said.

They settled the coffins in the parlor on the biers, head to head. "I'll get hay and water for the horses," the neighbor said, "if any others should come."

He straightened a hem of the blue cloth and turned to his wife, who was still rocking in the rib-backed wooden chair at the edge of the rug.

"We'll bury them out back in the grove. By the pines. In the morning?"

She nodded her head. "They'll be no gathering. If that Reverend comes by, I'll tell him so."

"I'd be doing all these things alone?"

"Yes," she said, "you would."

"There'll be no other time for this," he told her. "If any regret should come...."

She lifted a hand to stop him. He ran his palm along one wooden box, then the other.

"Suit yourself."

She heard the door slam behind him. Beyond the grove, across the ticking fields, a late afternoon sun, what was left of it, stained the parlor yellow. And behind the parlor and the barn, corn still smoldered which the boys had freshed picked a few days before. Now she could hear the wind whining through the drying crib.

Before any of the others arrived, she should have it done. She lifted from her chair and moved midway between the two sons, as not to favor either one.

"Damn you two," she said. "You wouldn't have it any other way." And she turned and went back to her rocking, to her whiskey, to that little place they had kept for her.

shake and burn

ellen dworsky

Turning her key in the lock one final time, she stands outside the house, now devoid of people and furnishings. She faces the deck—slightly slanted, the victim of California mudslides and earthquakes. Under three huge pine trees, an old kitchen table, waterlogged from too many winters outside, and three moldy kitchen chairs are pushed back from the table as if their occupants left just moments ago. The sun is setting behind the pines, glowing as fading sunlight filters through the branches. In a few hours the trees will be transformed again by the mist and fog that hangs between their needles in the hours of darkness.

Unwilling to leave, though there is no longer any reason to stay, her feet take her to the deck where she will sit one last time. Facing the brick and redwood house she wonders, *who will live here after I have gone? Where will I be a year from now?* She knows where Aaron will be. Forever frozen at twenty-seven. But she can still feel him here, can see his hazy outline sitting in the deck chair, and now, shimmering in the trees, sun shining through his long, silky hair.

She says goodbye, gets in her car and drives down Snake Boulevard. A mile of twists, curves and hairpin turns, onto Highway Thirteen, through the Caldecott tunnel. A tanker truck blew up one of the bores some years back in the hours before dawn. People died. She would have been passing through it when the tanker exploded but decided to stay the night in San Francisco instead of driving home. She did drive through the tunnel during the "Oakland Hills Firestorm"—the media's name for it. Nobody from California calls it that. She didn't catch fire that time either.

She drives through the suburbs on Highway 24 with the window down and the radio turned up loud. In Walnut Creek, she passes over the tallest connector ramp in the country and wonders what would happen if an earthquake hit in that instant. Would she and her car fly free? During the '89 quake she had been grocery shopping at Safeway. When the shaking subsided, she continued down the aisles, navigating around the broken jars of pasta sauce—thick blood and glass bones, littering the floor.

Merging onto the third busiest interchange in the United States, her car connects with Highway 680. She pays the toll at the Benicia Bridge and heads for Highway 80. This stretch of highway is a wind tunnel and she imagines her car is a plane hitting air pockets causing turbulence. Maybe she will crash to earth, a fiery wreck on the side of the road. Thirty miles outside of Sacramento, she stops for food and starts thinking about what put her on the road to Minnesota, The Land of Tall Blonde People.

As she pulls out of the parking lot, she looks in the rearview mirror, sees the vaporous form of Aaron sitting in the back seat surrounded by his possessions—the guitar he had hocked to buy crack, his yellow surfboard and wet suit, some of his favorite books: *Steppenwolf, The Painted Bird, Fear and Loathing in Las Vegas.* She stares at the road ahead, concentrating on the flat highway. When she looks in the rearview mirror again, he's still there, surrounded by the sunflowers they grew in the backyard. On the seat beside him, a bottle of Jack Daniels, a jar of weed, planted and harvested after the sunflowers had gone to seed, a syringe is in his hand. He injects himself with heroin that she knows killed him—three months ago, in the bathroom of a stranger's house. The stranger who sold him the heroin. She can't look. She stares straight ahead. Hands gripping the steering wheel, she accelerates until she's hurtling down the highway at 100 miles an hour. When she steals a glimpse in the rearview mirror, he's gone. She makes herself a deal. She'll only think when she smokes. One by one, she throws her cigarettes out the window. In her rearview mirror she watches them dance as the air catches them, and imagines she can see their glowing tips as they recede from view in the falling dark.

mood music

emily graves

When he was 15, he'd loved a girl named Summer. She lived in a basement bedroom to the right of the stairs next to the rumpus room. Everything in her room was black and red. He'd loved her big, white legs and the way she laid back in bed saying, "I don't care," after all of her stories. On summer days after band practice, he went with her to her house and they retreated into the dark back rooms of the basement, which had been built into a record library, and they touched all the cardboard in a religious way, flipping through stack after stack of records, rubbing their thumbs over the best covers, the most precious sounds.

"He has everything recorded from between 1968 and 1979," she said to him and he believed her.

"Benny, her dad, is a former DJ," he said to his parents, relishing the sound of the youthful name "Benny" and using words like "vinyl" and "recording studio" and all the small details to show his parents where they'd gone off-track into careers like "teacher" and "carpenter."

"Sure, but what does he do *now*?" one of them would ask, and Jorden could not answer.

The textures of the covers, the psychedelic grooves, the sounds of hands flipping records, of the needle's arm curving through the air and dropping onto the vinyl, blended into an enormous blanket thrown over the two of them in the post-band afternoons. It was cool and dark in the basement. There was only so much time to listen to the records, no time at all, really, and so they kept changing them after just a few seconds, listening to a minute of Jefferson Airplane and throwing on Television, Fairport Convention and Fleetwood Mac and Stevie Wonder and suddenly, at four o'clock, the flipping stopped when the front door opened and he always knew he'd stayed too long when he heard Georgette's shoes in the kitchen and her weary flop after the drag of the kitchen chair.

They turned the lights off quickly and went back to Summer's room which felt suddenly small and dank after the floor-to-ceiling rooms of records and the cool, concrete floors.

"Great. PMS is home," Summer said and dropped onto the bed sighing, "God, I don't care."

He never knew how to get out of the house then, how to leave without running into PMS. PMS loved him, was part of the problem, thought he was such a good influence, whereas Jorden saw her and wanted only to hear the screen door slap behind him, to feel the slick, black pavement under his feet as he sped for home. Summer picked up a glass of Pepsi that'd been left half-drunk on the floor and drank it. PMS came down the stairs and he could already see her swollen face, her octagonal glasses, her sighing blonde hair.

"Summer?" she said and tried to make it sound invitational, like a party or a dance.

"Mom!" she screamed. "Why do you keep bugging me!" she exploded into pre-crying whines, coming to an upright position on the edge of the bed, gripping the mattress with pained hands.

"Summer, we need to talk. Stay Jorden," she said to him, seeing his spine tensed and at the ready. And he shrank back onto Summer's bed and listened to their whispers and whimpers on the basement stairway, Summer's occasional teary yelp, until PMS called him out for a group hug saying, "Jorden, I think it would be good for you to be here for this too." During these rituals he braced himself and swore silently that he would always sleep alone, a sea of space around him on every side.

They formed a small circle, Summer still seething and sad and PMS gulping down air, regaining control, trying to be nice. Arms around each others shoulders, they moved forward, squeezing in and dropped arms again, looking at the floor, awkward and ashamed.

"Why do you go there?" Jorden's mother asked him. He didn't know exactly, but when he thought it over he saw in his mind the singles and 45's and LP's spinning around the word "DJ" and tiny black and red braids in a head of blonde hair, the smell of coffee, ripped off shorts and the big high tops Summer wore over athletic socks. When he thought it over, he felt soft.

All summer long, the band traveled to small, regional towns for parades and competitions. They wore dark, plum-colored, wool tuxedoes and tight hats with plumes and chinstraps. The instruments had choreographed movements that went with the music. Summer and Jorden both played trumpet. The band marched around town in shorts at 8 o'clock, three mornings a week, moving in sync up and down the hills, building up stamina for the parades. In late August, on a rare day when PMS and Benny both came home early, when Summer and Jorden were in the kitchen looking for Pop Tarts in the cupboard, Benny blew up. He snarled nastily at PMS and moved menacingly towards Summer as he screamed at both of them in the front hall. Jorden was cornered there for 20 minutes, the argument moving between him and escape. Benny slammed up the front stairs, saying to Jorden, "I'm sorry you had to see this, Jorden."

Summer came to school with a cigarette burn on her tennis shoe that year, she started riding in cars and turned a strange shade of yellow from lack of sleep, frustration and beer. They didn't talk anymore. At school, he was nobody.

Three years later, he saw her in the city at an outdoor music festival with a scrabbly boyfriend, a body full of tattoos and a pregnant belly. She said she was working at a club and her boyfriend was in a band. Her boyfriend put a skinny, protective arm around her and looked at Jorden passively. She talked to Jorden a minute, acting like having a baby was no big thing. Like none of it, tattoos, bars or belly were big. It was stupid, he realized later, but he just kept thinking, "But, you were so good at math. Why?" As if math was a reliable stimulus to pregnancy prevention hormones, as if math could take you somewhere, like a train or a scholarship. And she was too, good at math. Extraordinary. It came to her like magic.

please hold me the forgotten way

hannah shepard

His hair was dark and soft and curled a little because it was getting long. He must have thought it made him look too pretty. He disliked anything that made him attractive. He asked her to shave it. She liked the hair. She imagined touching it with her fingers and coming away with the sweet dark smell of his scalp on her hands. He left his wool hat at her house one night and she had slept with it next to her face. She hated giving it back, and crawled around her blankets at night trying to catch his smell as it disappeared.

She knew the drive to his house. She knew the trees she would pass, the fire hydrants, the dogs barking behind their fences. She knew where she would park, where the tires would hit the curb. She knew the way she would breathe and straighten her skirt, and the feel of the heat that would prickle down her arms and explode in her fingertips when she saw him through the kitchen window, coming to the door. He usually stared her down. Big dark eyes that studied her like a rare specimen. It wasn't exactly an adoring gaze. It was more one of bewilderment and concern. He greeted her like this the day she came to shave his head. He opened the door very cordially, one hand behind his back like the head waiter at a French restaurant, bowing slightly. She sensed his hand brush gently against her back as she came in. She moved too quickly for it to rest there.

"I have everything ready," he said severely, as if she had arrived to perform some critical operation.

She sat down at his kitchen table and smiled at him. The cold winter sunlight pooled in through the window and lit her hands folded on her lap, and she hoped he would remember her like this when he was an old man.

They went down the stairs out of the sunny kitchen and he followed close behind her. The bathroom in the basement was cold and lit by fluorescent lights. He knelt in front of her, and she thought that with him on his knees like this she could either love him or kill him. She could hold his head tenderly against her belly, or break his neck with one quick move. She could do both of these things with her hands.

The razor looked comical to her when she picked it up, hot pink against the cracked cement walls of the bathroom that were painted a dark fungal green. She ran the faucet. Waited for the water to heat up. Waited for it to be just right. She moved her wet soapy hands gently around his head, soaking his hair, around his ears, across his temples, to the nape of his neck. Some of it dripped down his face and he let it run to his chin and fall to the floor. She took the hair from his head in clumps, trying to ignore his back pressed against her legs, lifting and falling with his breath. And when she had washed the soap away his head was like a smooth ostrich egg. Porcelain white, shining and bare. His eyebrows stood out like black coal marks, alone on his face.

And she caught her breath when she saw the two of them in the mirror. The fluorescent light made their faces a sickly pale green and their eyes were underlined by dark circles. They both looked so tired. He looked sick and cold, and she looked as if she had been crying for him for a very long time.

people's delights

jarda cervenka

Cover the public housing with soot, surround it with a row of dirt-storing warehouses, break windows here and there, crack the asphalt on the roads and uproot a few hydrants, too. And don't forget to add a bar on each street, a bar where drinks are sold that can add rainbow colors to the drab of a day that resembles yesterday, tomorrow's twin, and on and on. And over this valley at the edge of the city build a bridge so immensely high that to the people gathering below it would seem to be a sliver of heaven.

***

They were carrying chairs out of the beer joint onto the street and on the sidewalk.

"Hurry up, you guys, hurry up!" The skinny one with the weasel's face urged them, his eyes highly glossed-over with eagerness and darting somewhere high up and back again to the entrance of the bar. The big one, with a ruddy, pitted nose on which the tangle of purple veins wrote the story of a breakfast alcoholic, carried two chairs, easily. There still were some muscles under his hippopotamic wrap of blubber. He could have been a trucker because of the claim on his cap: "No F-----g, No Trucking."

There was an old man with a wrinkled gray face in wrinkled, black suit, gesticulating spastically, pointing at spots for the chairs. "Put them in a row, facing that way, idiots!" He was bent sideways and forward, but the curvature of his back was not of hunchback severity, yet. Nobody paid attention to him and he seemed not to expect any. He championed his decrepitude with an occasional coughing spell.

The woman (it seemed to be a female), in her thirties or sixties, also advised. From time to time she would abandon her agitation and, with her fists buried where her waist used to be, elbows high, she would tilt her head backward and stare up. A smile would come to her face, failing to improve it.

"Let's put out the long table, too," the beer-bellied authority ordered from the doorway of the bar. "Move your ass; it could happen any minute!" He sported a sailor's cap, pushed back to provide him, perhaps, a carefree image. His shirt-sleeves were rolled up and one knew the ropes of the muscles of his forearm did not acquire the bulk only by lifting beer mugs. The skin-fold flapping from his chin to the bottom of the red neck enhanced his weighty authority, as it does to a male iguana. The table was carried out in an instant. Then the toughie brought out six full mugs, three in each hand, spilling the foam only. Some pickled herring and pickled sausages with onion were brought onto the table; the bread, sliced thick on wooden plate, was on the house.

A few customers brought out more chairs onto the sidewalk, while not neglecting their beer. One held a shot glass with clear fluid. When they drank from their mugs, tilting their heads backward, their heads remained tilted back while their mugs went down on the table. The upturned eyes of all customers seemed fervent. Some narrowed them in a smile; most appeared eager, in anticipation. The mood was becoming festive with the clinking of beer-glasses, contented chatter, the mumble and mutter of tongues made sluggish by drink. The ageless woman pointed above her again, chuckling. "Takes her time," she said. "She takes her goddamn time."

The sun, having seen enough for today, hurried to hide behind the roof of the tallest warehouse. The air was dead. It was hot and steamy, a climate of violence for some, of lethargy for others and, possibly, of suffering which had became unbearable, for one.

She was not alone on the bridge. An ambulance blocked traffic in one lane; patrol cars rotated their blue electronic fireflies. A police psychologist talked to her with trained calmness from a few steps away. She balanced on the railing, holding onto a steel cable.

How old was she? Was she pretty? Was she smart? Had she lost family or a lover? Was her despair irreparable? Or was her body diseased? We do not know, and if we knew, it would be another long story, because every human story must be long if told in truth, and a story of self-destruction should be contained in thousand pages.

She wore a loose black frock that would stretch in flight like monstrous raven's wings. The wind blew her long hair over her face, but in the fall the hair would follow like the tail of a comet. If she took the lethal plunge would she make a sound, other than the swishing pitch of the wind? Or would she fall as silently as an owl flies across the moon? But are we sure that she devised the free fall of her free will? To free herself, would she descend into oblivion now? Why was she waiting? The sun had fallen already.

***

The only thing certain was that the people down on the street were ready. The beer still flowed, but the supply of pale pickled sausages with plenty of onion had been exhausted by those sitting in delightful anticipation.

the mystery formations

jay orff

The canyon that holds these formations can't be seen from the highway. Look for signs that point to a road that leads to a parking area with a commanding overlook and trailheads that lead through the curious stone outcroppings below the steep hills. Along the path are markers that explain how it is believed these curiosities were formed, the outcome of an unusual combination of hot springs, ice ages, and the mineral content of the bedrock. There is another explanation, one that gained notoriety recently. Across from the entrance of the park, on the other side of the highway, a weathered billboard above a rundown gas station proclaims it is the home of "The Shocking Truth." For a small admission fee you can enter the cramped and hot building and look over documents that prove, according to the owner, that the park across the road is a sham. Apparently, so the conspiracy theory goes, in the distant past the founders of the town agreed to create the formations and then destroy all evidence of their construction. Hanging on the walls in this former filling station is the marginalia that escaped the purge. There are no plans or diagrams. Instead, it is a collection of notes, love letters, calendars with dates circled all bearing the same cryptic words ("abutment", "evacuation", "bituminous" and others), which, if one accepts these words as code, reveal a covert plan to create the park. A few scientists have written about the unlikely and precise order of the Mystery Formations and the ensuing debate has made the park all the more popular. You should arrive early in the day if you want to avoid the crowds arguing about the wonder of nature versus the ingenuity of man. And if you want a T-shirt from The Shocking Truth, visit before June, they are always out of stock by July.

ride to paradise

jessy greene

"Any truckers going southbound on I-90?"

The CB receiver spits back static and a crackling war torn voice, "Big Red here, I can take you as far as Maryland little girl, and you won't find a nicer ride."

"I ain't no little girl and WE are just looking for a ride... A Ride. Get it?"

"Yeah, whatever. I am leaving in five if you want to go with me. You won't find no trouble here."

Michelle and I ran out of the diner, dodging lakes of mud. Rain pounded the leather jackets on our backs in a loud, spastic rhythm. We had packed a knife for protection but no umbrella for the rain. In the distance a big rig was flashing her lights and blowing a lonesome horn. By the time we reached the sweet, cherry Peterbilt everything we owned was soaking wet and splattered with mud, but Michelle giggled as she pulled me up into the roaring beast.

"Hello lovelies." Big Red yells over the rattle of his freshly ignited engine. He gives us a quick glance as he shoves the stick into gear.

"Hold on girls."

We are off. Our journey has begun. The cab is mint, full of chrome and leather with a front seat big enough for Michelle and I. We settle in. We are wet, cold and homeless but as I push gently against her side nothing else matters. I feel safe. I am dizzy with anticipation of what lies on the road ahead and determined to leave behind the baggage that brought me here. Life seems real for a change. I can hear Big Red's strange voice asking familiar questions but I tune him out leaving the small talk to Michelle. The rain cries down the window pane, morphing into endless rivers. We are so high, going so fast it feels as if we are floating above the freeway. We were breaking from the pack, leaving behind our dirty dog town so few have escaped from.

And this time it was for good.

I'd been running for years and I was barely 18. But I never made it far from where I was born. I didn't want to go it alone, and every time I planned to leave with a man it got fucked up. Michelle had been my only real family since we were kids. We were two months away from high school graduation but things around town were heating up. I had bad habits, bad ass lovers, bad judgment, and a lot of people were not happy with me. After a few close calls I became convinced it was either get out of town or get killed.

"Wake up, Jessy." Michelle hits me hard on the arm.

I sit up and try to focus fast. Suddenly I see the truck is swerving toward the edge of the road, I turn to see our driver's head slung back like he was a dead man.

"BIG RED!" Michelle and I scream. His head jerks back to life.

"What? Damn, did I nod out for a minute?" He grabs the wheel and in a heartbeat the truck lunges, skids, and is back on track. We didn't sleep much after that, Big Red had some speed and we all thought it would be a good idea to stay awake.

The rain stopped when we hit Maryland. It was time to find a new ride. We had never seen such a big truck stop. You could find just about anything there. We took showers and bought some pot off a kid we met at the diner.

"Are you girls up to no good?" A gray haired, wiry man smirked at Michelle as she was shoving the pot into her bra.

"It's just some pot...and what do you care?" Michelle spat at him.

“Ok then...well, enjoy.” He turned to leave.

“Wait, which direction are you going?” Michelle stuck her elbow into my ribs as I spoke.

"Down South, way down to the tip of Florida." The man replied.

Michelle heard my thoughts as if I had spoken them.

“We're going to Daytona, could we catch a ride?” Her tone was suddenly much sweeter.

“It would be my pleasure.”

The Green Beret introduced himself. He was a retired military officer who loved the open road and drove a big rig to pass the time.

“I'm actually headed down the west coast but I have no problem with a little detour.”

The Green Beret let us smoke pot in the cab and play Aerosmith really loud. It was a beautiful ride. Spring broke early as the dismal Northeast faded into the lush Southern landscape.

We cheered as we crossed the Florida state line. We made it. Daytona Beach, April 18, Michelle's eighteenth birthday. The Green Beret drove his 18-wheeler off the interstate and right up to the edge of the ocean.

“We won't forget you.” Michelle leaned over and gave him a hug. He slipped a piece of paper into her hand.

“Here's my number. Call me if you decide to head

back east, and I will come and get you. Please be careful, girls."

We waved goodbye and turned around to face the ocean breeze. It was a breathtaking sight. We were momentarily blinded by the water reflecting off the hotrod cars and oil covered, muscle bound bodies spread out on the sand. We had made it seventeen hundred miles in two and a half days without sticking out our thumbs. But now it was time, we had to find a place to clean up and put our stuff. We hitched a ride into downtown Daytona and found a youth hostel where we rented a locker and a hot shower. Fresh and ready for Saturday night we walked out of the hostel into the brilliant neon lights of the Daytona strip.

One by one, beautiful, long haired boys in muscle cars blaring heavy metal cruised by. Palm trees bent over in the warm breeze, welcoming us to the party. Michelle and I grabbed eath other's arms in delight and danced off into the crowded street, easily blending into the mass of lost youth.

Disappearing into paradise.

the gulf

k.c. hanson

I've been having my boys hit beaches, duck and cover, cut and roll, fire and maneuver, fire and movement, *this is how you take a fucking hill* for months now—practicing mostly on this damned boat, pointing real guns at each other and yelling *Buddha Buddha,* which should be really funny to Christians but they don't get it—fucking misguided children—but I couldn't train them for this. They're all white now, scared, and look like they might piss jizz and shit themselves. You'd swear we were going to live fire some tanks in our skivvies, and we might—you have to know that—but that's not what's bothering them. That wouldn't bother them at all. These boys, my boys, were born (if not born again) to jackoff and burn tanks; snap, jack, and burn the fandango: *I breathed the syph brother, no clanky tintopped mother steppin' on my britches.* They just couldn't do the math.

None of them. So when I said, *We got seven mags each and each hold thirty smackers or three loaders of ten, so you could say twentyone or twoten,* nobody gave a fuck. Only I do when they don't know. They just kept stuffing bullets 'til they were full. *It's twoten, Smoke, you can trust me on that.* Then I turned to two of the hoodboys and asked *How many bullets did each guy get off at Normandy?* They *dunno.* At least they say they *dunno* but when I say *nine* they don't seem a bit surprised, like the difference between nine and two-hundred-and-ten is either too tiny to matter or they're planning on doing a whole lot more killing here than got done there. I guess we'll find out. I'm carrying twoten too. And a map even though I don't know wherethefuck I'm going. Call it my baby blanket; it makes me feel better.

Numbnuts took a prybar to a grenade crate and there was a lot of *oohs* and *aahs* and *cool mothers* going on until I started hammering the clip backs on my helmet to seat the rounds. That's the traditional way to make sure you'll be shooting back. And my boys, the ignorant fucks, came back sobered to do the same, so I didn't have to say too much about that, which is good, and just about the grenades.

We each got four—heavier in my hand than I imagined even though I've held them before, maybe for the potential more than sheer poundounce weight; fucking grenades, they bother me. I bend the pins over good and bothways, tight, like a religion: any bomb strapped to me better for damn sure not go off. I check everyone else's but they don't seem interested. They're young. Grenades and bullets are for the enemy whoeverthefuck they might be, and won't hurt them. No shit. So I'm just mothering them, *poo poo pee do,* like I'm getting cereal for my little sister when I check their gear. These are *tough motherfuckers*. They even say so.

I yell that *I'm up* but check them once again because the first time is never enough when you're leading little ducklings through angry waters and they are jabberjawing *yo yo* whateverthefuck and *yolmes*—about how *def* and *dude* and the hoodboys hiphop about south Compton with the Mex from New York. I got no idea what the fuck it means but I laugh anyway because not even God Almighty could fuck up enough to put this crew together.

I'm the one who leads the line up the stairwell *make way* onto the quarterdeck clanking with all this extra shit. Death is heavy. But morale is high—*somebody's in for an asskickin', shee-it*—because Hotrod the Mex says so, and I'm smoking because who the fuck's going to tell me not to?

Eventually I'm up, signing for *atropine* and *two-panchloride* which I guess you shoot in your leg when you're fucked and then Doc E. at the next table hands me a little tube, silver on the ends with a needledropper. He doesn't look so good. I lean over to sign and initial for *morphine sixteenmgs* and stutterstop—blankeyed—Doc E. looking. He says *It's half now and half later if you take one,* I know he means a bullet, and then he says, *but I've been letting everybody know that if you take the whole works it's all over*. I thank him even though he is staring at the sea. It seems like the thing to do. His career's over for saying it. You can't just tell troops how to end it all. I know and he knows I know and he's a *Good fucking Doc.*

So now I watch the braveboys turn ghostwhite, even the black ones, tails tucked under their nuts, coming from the tables holding not the enemy's death in their imaginations, but their own.

this is what would have happened

kathryn knudson

I'm pretty sure this is what would have happened.

He'd be a colonel by now, retired. Shoes polished and posture strong. His tastes would be refined but hardly extravagant, so while people knew he'd been away, they also knew he still fit in, as much as he ever did. He would have returned to where he grew up, settling in a compact house on the north edge of town, close enough to farmland to look over what he'd gotten to overlook.

She would be a linguist writing papers that would be read by people with initials tripping after their names. Graduate students would highlight her sentences and footnote her in papers en route to their initials. She'd write under her maiden name, taken back after the divorce.

He would have become a collector; items gathered from his various stations. Rugs and trinkets, cricket bats and baskets, and his favorite, a weaving of dancing women. He would have Korean pottery and beer steins no one drank from and postcards he didn't send in boxes in his basement and attic. Remnants of his travels washed up into his present.

Her three children, Egyptian on their father's side, would have been raised to do their own laundry, even the youngest, a son. On rare occasion, she'd share stories remembered from Brazil, especially of her husband before he was her husband. Her head would tilt back with laughter, descriptions slipping into Portuguese. Inevitably, she'd run into memories of when he was her husband and the laughter would break, closing her off again. She would be more walled away when speaking English than when reminiscing in Portuguese, a language her children wouldn't know.

Both of them would have been what people describe as accomplished and give generously to charities and keep to themselves just enough. She too would have drifted back to farms and gravel roads and three-block long main streets. And they would have known each other as you do in small towns, neighbors who pass greetings at the post office.

And possibly one day, while holding the bank door open for her he would have felt what she felt, a moment when both thought they glimpsed, almost remembered, a life different from this one. And in the second it would take for her to step past him both would have shaken this off, the moment less forgotten than ignored because neither of them would believe in this kind of thing.

the glory of teamwork

kevin carollo

Joanna and I were about ten fee away when we heard her body hit the water. By then, each of us had silently decided to start hating ourselves for wanting to come to Loredo Taft in the first place. Now either Sue Langdon was being tormented and perhaps worse by a bunch of eighth-grade boys, or a bunch of popular people were feeling all cool for going skinny dipping.

Neither of our hippie parents believed in the mission statement of Loredo Taft, or the parent-teacher conference handout about the "character-building three days on the privately owned forest preserve of Taft's 800 acres." They didn't teach us farm math in the suburban schools, so I can't say how much 800 acres is in length times width equals area, but if the community wanted to pony up for a couple days of teamwork and leadership lessons in the woods, I figured that was as good enough reason to get out of school as any. So did Joanna.

It's not like we were going to sneak away to the mall to get tattoos when everybody went to sleep. We figured this was as woods as Illinois was going to get, and we might as well see them before they too became another industrial park. Both nights of the trip we would have Night Walks, where we were supposed to shine flashlights on the small bits of nature nestling in the tree bark, and periodically track other Packs as if we were fighting for our lives across enemy lines.

To listen to the school counselors, who clearly needed to get into nature more themselves, it sounded almost educational. One day Joanna and I hoped to work for minimum at Great America or become summer camp counselors in another state, and this was just the one way the public school system intended to prepare us for our future in child development.

Our hippie parents knew firsthand what we were signing up for. They had *been* to Loredo Taft when *they* were in eighth grade, so in *their* minds they were trying to save us a *whole* bunch of angst and conformist crap about working as a team for the Man. They knew about the rank dorms that we would line up in front of each morning. In a "character-building simulation of military discipline," they had Reveille at 7 a.m. with bugle horn and inspirational thought for the day. I, for one, didn't expect the food to be as bad as it was 25 years ago, but they still don't grill the cheese. They put butter on white bread and then add slices of American cheese, but they won't grill it. Each bowl of iceberg lettuce had one slice of tomato in it, just as Mom had foretold. Things got worse at dinnertime.

Peter Fanfaron broke his hand when he slipped and fell into a dorm window. Erik Dischmann took a dump on Michael Janus' head and threw up in the boys' dorm sink afterward. Buffy and Dom were rumored to have done "everything but" out by the reeds and scrub of the No Trespassing Zone. Several members of the cheerleading squad were rumored to have gotten drunk on wine coolers and made out with each other like on cable. And a whole bunch of gross stuff I'm not even going to mention.

On Thursday, Joanna and I split off from Squirrel Pack during the last Night Walk. The different shades of black at night were actually kinda cool, but for a supposedly secluded area there were too many jerkoffs on this glorified field trip to truly appreciate them. Joanna had her camera, and I had brought the cigarettes.

We started to smoke. "This sucks."

"Agreed."

Before too long, we heard a stampede of Badger Pack jocks yell "splash her" and "c'mon guys, get her wet."

Sue Langdon protested, but didn't sound too convincing. We couldn't hear the other girls from their Pack, but they may have been there, watching. Sue Langdon already has big tits and is rumored to be a slut, perhaps one because of the other, I'm not sure. I was glad to be in her Pack, because it felt embarrassing for all us girls to see her so macked on by the guys who were always trying to feel her up or make her take her top off or whatever. It was like no one could really be her friend either, you know, so I felt some kind of connection there. Not that I would ever talk to her or anything, but that's just my thing I'm dealing with right now. Other people.

"Joanna, do something," I whispered.

"What do you want me to do?" she asked. "I'm trying to get them in focus." She muttered something smart about infrared lenses and embedded journalism, and I just let it ride. We inched our way to the group quietly, and I could feel my heart pounding like the Indian drumming we learned in school, only much faster.

It became really spooky as we approached, as if the early crickets had taken over the entire soundtrack. The silence was worse than the laughing. I think I heard Sue giggling and saying "no way." Then her "no don't" splash was followed by other splashes, and boys and girls talking about nothing. Everyone dove in, and came up as stupid and gross as always.

I didn't expect Joanna to shout, "Sue, we hope you're okay!" But she did.

No one said anything at first, then Brock and/or Casper said, "what's up with her?" more to the swamp or lake than to us. We had already started to run full steam toward the dorms.

So now I have a cut on my left knee that probably won't ever go away.

In the morning, there are cornflakes and a sad view of a gulch of dying trees. Joanna and I had gotten up early to take pictures of the mist, but there wasn't any. Now we have to get through a stupid two-hour scavenger hunt before getting on the school bus for three hours.

Our wish that Squirrel Pack doesn't have to combine forces with Badger Pack comes true. Instead of looking for leaves and twigs and stuff, Joanna takes photos of my playing dead over a kind of ridge with a twisted tree poking out. She takes blurry pictures of backgrounds and crystal-clear close-ups of bark, branches, my cut.

We don't say anything on the trip home. She plays with her cell phone and I have an iPod. The weather is so not cooperating. It reminds us of how long and lonely another month of school can be.

As we pull into the parking lot, I chant some Siouxsie

and the Banshees lyrics I downloaded: "Be a carcass / be a dead pork / be limplessly in love." To no one in particular, Joanna says, "Be all that you can be."

In the future, we will move to the city, get jobs, stop eating meat, and become different people. So there's that to look forward to. And now I guess we have a weekend without homework.

go to hell, franklin

kim teeple

Franklin bought it not once, but twice.

He died the first time when he jumped off the Mendota Bridge into the Mississippi River during a blizzard. I could have told everyone it was an accident, he couldn't see, was snow blind, but God knows I didn't owe him any favors.

"No, Franklin," I said to the air, the space around me, "you're going to have to live with your decision."

That night, lying in bed, I saw a hulking shadow near the bedpost. After thirty years of living with the bastard, I recognized my husband—deceased husband—Franklin.

"Go to Hell, Franklin!" I shouted toward the shadow at the foot of the bed.

I flopped back down and pulled the covers over my head. From underneath the blanket, I could hear a muffled voice, "I'm in Hell already, I'm still lookin' at you!" I pulled the covers down to my chin and peeked out. The shadow at the foot of the bed solidified, took form; first, his round, nearly bald head, then his shoulders, his big belly, and last came his bowed legs.

I sat up. "We gotta redeem you, get you penance for your sin," I told him.

There was no way I was going to go on living with him. "I'll call Father Dolney in the morning."

I woke up to the sound of burping. "Wha's the matter?" I asked him. "You only get gas at night when you're worrying about something." "My stomach hurts," he moaned. I wondered if it was too early in the morning to call the rectory. "If you're worried about confession to save your soul, Father Dolney knows you committed suicide. Good-Mary-mother-of-Jesus, Franklin. He presided over your funeral."

"Boopkins..." When he was alive and feeling frisky, Franklin called me Boopkins. I turned my back, faced the wall, and pretended to fall back asleep.

"Who came to my funeral?" Franklin sighed behind me, "That's all I was going to ask you." I almost felt sorry for him.

"I'm sleeping, Okay? Let me sleep."

****

In the morning, Franklin hovered around the kitchen until I thought it a reasonable hour to call over to the church. He was standing too close, trying to listen in. My side felt like it was buried in wet sand.

Judy Deeks answered the phone at the Rectory. Her dentures slipped when she talked.

"Father 'olney is on shabbatical for the resh of the week."

I slammed the receiver back into place. Franklin and I would simply have to make do till then.

"I'm going to the library," I told him. Franklin was sniffing at the coffee.

"I can't smell the coffee. Yours gave me heartburn, but I liked the smell of it." All-the- Saints-in-Heaven-above, I had a haunt with gripes.

"I'm getting books on exorcism," I said. The screen door banged shut after me.

When I came back from the library, all the lights in the house were on.

"Look what I can do." Franklin grinned, or tried to—his mouth wavered when he smiled.

The dishwasher was running, and the empty coffee

pot was cracked. The air conditioning was blasting and so were the television and the stereo. My blow dryer in the bathroom was blowing, and my hot curlers were on, too. The whole house whirred with the hum of electrical appliances.

I set the books on the kitchen table and banged my forehead on the pile.

After a short while I got up and started shutting things off. Franklin followed me around the house like a sullen child. I flicked off the coffee pot; the light was still lit. I swiped at the button again. Franklin chuckled across the room. "Knock it off, Franklin," I yelled. The light went out.

Franklin read over my shoulder as I thumbed through the books. He jabbed his fat finger into the page, it went through the words. "This is about getting rid of demons. I'm not a demon." A cold gust of air raised the hairs on the back of my neck.

"Could have fooled me," I snapped. Franklin took his finger out of the book, he looked hurt. I felt bad. I tried to touch his hand, forgetting I couldn't really touch him, then he was gone. I heard our radio go on in the bedroom.

The rest of the week we bickered and argued as usual, and Franklin drove the wits out of me discovering his new found spectral abilities.

Aside from being able to turn things on and off, Franklin was delighted to discover he could project his voice through the radio. At first he wailed and moaned like a ghost. Then he started singing along—his own personal karaoke machine—and the song choices were endless. He flipped from rock and roll, to country, and even opera. When he started singing with Pavarotti, I was about ready to kill him. "God-almighty-and-Angel's-trumpets, find the oldies station," I hollered, but I couldn't help smiling.

***

When it was time to call Father Dolney again, Franklin leaned over my shoulder and listened in. By now though, I was used to his strange damp presence.

Father Dolney wasn't convinced.

"Bobbie, I recommend you join Mrs. Hillcock's grieving widow's group every third Sunday in the church basement."

Mabel Hillcock had been playing the grieving widow card for seven years. And for the last six years, she'd spent every Friday night at Ted Bagley's house.

Father finally consented to making a house call.

I hung up the phone and Franklin was grinning. His mouth shimmered like heat waves on a hot road.

"Father Dolney thinks you've gone batty," Franklin laughed. "He thinks you're a bible verse short of a homily."

"Shut up, Franklin," I said. But I knew he was right.

An hour later, Father Dolney knocked.

Franklin opened the screen door.

"Ted Bagley is handy. I can send him over to fix this latch." Father swung the screen door back and forth jerking it away from Franklin.

He told me he wanted to get started right away due to the fact he'd been on sabbatical and was behind.

Franklin and I followed Father through the house as he went from room to room muttering prayers from a little black book, splashing holy water in the sign of the cross every few paces. Franklin lifted a silver flask out of Father's deep pocket and whispered "whiskey" in my ear, then slipped it back in. I wanted to tell him he didn't have to whisper, I was the only one who could see and hear him.

I winked at him instead.

In the bedroom, Father Dolney stood at the end of the bed, in the same spot where Franklin had materialized. He started chanting in Latin. I'd been watching Father and hadn't noticed Franklin was fading.

His big belly became transparent, and a dark shadow replaced where his upper body had been. "Franklin," I shouted, "Franklin, no!" Father Dolney stopped his singsong and opened his eyes. "Please Father," I begged, "please stop." But it was too late.

Franklin's head was disappearing: his chin, then his earlobes, his mouth, nose, and forehead—all that was left was a tuft of gray hair, then that was gone. I could still see the dark shadow of his outline, just like on the first night when he came back to me. I wanted to run into his shadow, feel him again.

The shadow floated apart, separated and disappeared.

Father Dolney left one of Mabel's grieving widow pamphlets on the counter.

That night, I peered in the dark toward the end of the bed, hoping to see my Franklin. I turned on the radio wanting to hear his voice. I heard a door slam and I jumped out of bed and called out to him. But it was nothing.

I called Mabel the next day.

a small, dark, roaring moon

lon otto

He saw this once on *Nova*—Egyptian laborers levering an obelisk while an Englishman tossed pebbles underneath it. The laborers levered from there, more pebbles, more levering, gradually raising the impossibly heavy pillar above the desert floor. Isaiah has no laborers, but he has a long iron prybar, and buckets of rock sifted from the flower bed he's been digging, and a 12 by 10 by 30 inch object he discovered at the bottom of his excavation. He thinks it must be worked limestone left over from the pre-Civil War stone house next door.

Across the street, Somali kids are playing basketball in front of Howard Withers' garage, lots of cussing, which means Howard isn't home. "*Hell* no!" a boy shouts when somebody shoots, a charm against scoring. It apparently works, for soon others take it up, "*Hell* no!" punctuating the slapping of the ball on pavement and the crash against rickety backboard and the roar and shudder of a helicopter flying somewhere close by.

Where Isaiah is working, between his driveway and the old stone house, the ground is so full of junk, he's decided to dig everything out, separate the rubble—bricks, clinkers, medicine bottles, rocks, chunks of concrete, an iron pipe, cow bones—then return the good soil amended with compost. He was about to leave off digging and start the backfilling this evening when his shovel struck what turned out to be this block, not much larger than carry-on luggage, but incredibly heavy.

He levers with the prybar, shoves stones under the block. When he straightens to ease his back, two little Hmong girls are leaning on the fence beneath his dwarf cherry tree. "Mister," one of them says, "are we supposed to eat these fruit?"

He thinks about the question. "They're sour."

"We don't mind," the other one declares.

"Help yourself."

The girls stand on tiptoe, select a handful each from the low-bending branches, glancing over their shoulders to see how closely he's watching them. A boy chases the basketball across the street, looks over at Isaiah, who nods, and grabs some cherries from a branch that's out of reach for the Hmong girls. "Man," he says, "these are *good,"* but doesn't pick any more.

The roar of the helicopter hasn't gone away. Isaiah climbs out of his excavation and walks into the street to look for it, and several of the basketball players point until he catches sight of it in a gap between trees, higher than he'd expected, and maybe a dozen blocks to the north and east. He waits to see which direction it goes, but though the sound seems to advance and recede, the helicopter hangs there in the evening sky as fixed as a moon. A small, dark, roaring moon. The Hmong girls suddenly run away, leaving a trail of glistening cherries rolling on the sidewalk.

Isaiah would get out his bicycle and ride over to see what's going on that holds the helicopter so obsessively, but he promised Sara he'd remove the mountain of dirt heaped in the driveway so she can get her car into the garage tonight. Recovering the antique limestone block has thrown him off schedule.

He has it almost to the lip of the hole, prybar and perilous stack of rubble jammed underneath. On *Nova,* white men are always proving how ancient people did amazing things. Sometimes their ideas are ridiculous, and other white men with competing theories mock them, like the poor dope claiming the Inca cut stone with sunlight concentrated by parabolic mirrors of gold, who couldn't even get straw to smolder.

The lever and pebble technique works fine, however, and as darkness falls Isaiah wrestles the block out of the hole onto his driveway. He's dead tired, but pleased he managed the feat without crushing any of his extremities or having the pry bar spring back and break his jaw.

The helicopter, he realizes, has finally gone away. His friend Lynette tells him about it the next day. A woman had been discovered in a car's trunk, that was what the helicopter was doing there. Neighbors had noticed the smell, called the police. "I couldn't believe it," Lynette says, "people hanging out of windows, climbing out on their porch roofs, everybody trying to get a look." She shakes her head. "I wouldn't want to look at no dead body in a trunk, poor thing."

"I thought of going over to see what was happening," Isaiah says.

She looks at him. "You did no such thing."

"I thought about it."

"A dead *body*?"

"I didn't know what it was."

"What it was, was a dead body in some murdering fool's *trunk*."

In the light of day, Isaiah discovers after hosing it off that the limestone block he salvaged with such effort is not stone at all, but concrete. He takes the prybar and uses it to tumble the block back into the hole, then starts burying it again, a pointless secret at the bottom of his new flowerbed's rich, deep soil.

the thing about rain

martin brick

"Describe the rain to me," he asks.

"I don't want to," I tell him. "You don't really want me to," but he says he does. He says I describe everything so poetically. I tell him he'll regret it, like how the geese ceased to fascinate him after he watched that documentary. In theory it should have made their migration all the more impressive, but in actuality it took all the wonder out of his gaze. And now he rarely looks skyward when he hears their droning honks in October.

He kisses the back of my neck, as if to encourage my words. The neck thing doesn't work like it used to. He can kiss my neck, my knee, my hand, ankle or nipple. I'm not wired that way anymore. I don't remember goose bumps (is there any connection to geese? To autumn? To chilled air? I don't know, should I care if I spoil his rain? I guess not.)

"The thing about rain is that it is a layered sound, and

most people don't give it that credit. You have to listen to the rain the way you watch a Hitchcock film. Most people zero in on the sound that it makes against the window or the roof. They'll note the banal drum taps. But listen. There is a distant white noise, like crowd applause on an old BBC recording of classical music performance. Yehudi Menuhin is playing violin and that rain is what comes at the end of a movement: steady, dignified, poorly mic-ed praise. That old analog sound.

"No, the most interested listeners of rain listen for what is close. There is often a burrowing sound. Usually near a door or a window – there is water dribbling off a porch, running down a corner. I don't understand the physics, but there is always some leaking that creates the sound of a mouse chewing."

He is quiet and listening as we lie on the couch. Its back faces a big picture window. My back is to his chest. His ears are piqued. His hand on my hip. My hand impatiently circulating, on top of his, at my hip. It is a slight reach backward that is awkward and tires my arm. My other arm is folded up under my chin and fallen asleep. Close to the edges, I'm all off-balance. With the slightest nudge from him I could tumble flat on my face on the floor. Honestly, I just want the couch to myself.

We're both silent for too long. Thunder mediates.

"How would you describe that?" he asks.

"How would you?" I counter.

"You're the one who's good at this."

"It's completely subjective. How am I better than anyone else?"

"Do you remember our first time?"

"You mean the first time we—?"

"Yeah. At that hotel."

"Of course I do."

"I remember that afterward you began describing the smell of soap, because someone in the next room was running the shower and you could smell the soap. I've never heard odor of soap described any way but 'soapy' or 'clean,' but you, you called it the product of an old man whittling cedar, soaking the shavings in spring rain, and drying them on a sunny windowsill. What an odd thing to talk about at that time, but your attention and praise and joy...It made me love you so much right then. I knew that if you always had that mind, that acuity, I would always love you."

"So describing the thunder will make you love me now?"

"I love you now, it's just..." He's in a corner.

Nota Bene: I married as a virgin, just as much by accident as by intent. The right combination of fear, shyness, idealism, enamoration at a young age, and desire to commit. It was perfect. It is one thing I don't like to use words for – they are inadequate – but everything fit. Everything felt right. Natural.

Another round of thunder. Very low. Very distant. Very sustained. He makes an attempt to describe it. A pandering effort to entice me. He compares it to the sound of a bowling ball. But the thunder doesn't really have that substance. You can tell a bowling ball has weight. Some thunder will shake a house, but this doesn't. It reminds me of high school, taking a test, the room is quiet and someone in the hall is pushing an AV cart. The thunder is the sound of the casters on the floor, an empty hall, a rattling tin shelf. It's very weak thunder tonight.

Of course, maybe it's just me.

Nothing is quite so vibrant anymore. The rain not so enhancing, the neck kisses not so electric. And I date this dulling of my senses back to—now here's the ironic thing—I date it back to the day I said "I want to know more." It wasn't meant to be a declaration of rebellion. Certainly not infidelity. But just a desire to feel less trapped.

Does it really matter how I met the guy? Does it really matter what his name was or what he did for a living? What matters is that at first I never considered it flirting, but within a few weeks I found him between my legs and I found real philosophical depth in the panting of my breath and found real charm in his classic-style t-shirts and his loose grip on cigarettes.

Amazing how quickly it wore thin. One day it was all about the new things. After sex he likes to walk around and look out the window. Not like he's checking for a husband's car or anything, but looking out the way people look at art or watch a little league game. Arms crossed across his chest. Tilted head. Rocked back and forth on his feet and then he'd talk. Dreaming stuff, usually. Like the type of house he'd build. By hand. And the orchard that would surround it. I found great wonder in watching the way his leg muscles would flex when he walked and in listening to the timbre of his voice. A week later all those things seemed so childish and uninteresting.

What killed my desire to know more? I can't say. Maybe it was that he was somewhat childish, slightly egotistical, or a fuzzy James Dean photocopy. Copy of a copy, really. Or may it was the little note my husband left in my pocket. "You are my sunshine O." Nothing poetic, but nothing too sappy. To the point and for no reason. That'll instill a little old-fashioned guilt.

So I try to forget this has happened and go back to the way things used to be. You'd think I would appreciate my husband more and savor his kisses. Savor everything. But nothing about him or anything is as good as it once was. Finding out about Santa. Learning Oz wasn't a real place. This is what it all feels like. Everything touching my senses is a veneer, and really less interesting underneath.

tainted

maureen aitken

On the first day of jury duty at the Hennepin County Government Center, Anne interpreted the lack of metal detectors as a clear advertisement for open, public rampage.

With the Conceal and Carry Law in full effect, Anne sat in the crammed room and eyed the men wearing hunting caps. The women with the hostile knitting needles didn't fool Anne, either. Who didn't own a gun? Anne, whose weapon potential consisted of a bike helmet and a purse with linty pennies.

A court employee lectured the packed room about the indecency of chewing gum, reading, and talking while in the presence of a judge. A woman from the jury pool yelled out: "I have kids and no sitter, for crying out loud."

"I have kids, too," a woman shouted.

A man stood up: "I'll lose my job if I am called."

Try as she might to maintain her sobriety, hope flooded Anne's heart. The crowd could murder the court employee – tear him limb from limb – then whoever was not charged with murder would be judged as tainted by the experience and sent home.

But the employee lectured (while reeling from his heels to his tip toes) that those with special circumstances could line up and proclaim their plight to the court administrator. Potential jurors heaved themselves at the door, and the remaining hoard sat quietly stewing in their own lack of vision.

She thought, *God, don't let me be called.*

After the lecture, Anne took her purse and bike helmet and found an empty seat in a nearby jury box. She kicked her feet up on the faux wood banister and tried unsuccessfully to read her book, *The Trial,* which seemed like such a good choice at home, but now only duplicated the same toneless human condition.

On and on she went, studying the 1970s brown, plywood, the dull caramel carpeting; the indifferent walls. She whispered to them, as if sitting in the cup of an ear, "Don't let me be called."

Suddenly, she could feel herself turning into one of those people, those people who bothered other people who wanted to read their books.

Anne tried to stop herself. She gripped her helmet.

The second day passed. People were called into juries, others got out. One man said to a woman, "He should have gotten off."

The woman shrugged: "The defense attorney didn't do a good job."

Anne wanted to borrow someone's gun and shoot that woman dead.

Instantly, Anne became one of those people: "Excuse me," Anne said to the woman reading a romance novel. "Do you think many people get off these jury duties?"

"Some, sure," she said. She was a kind woman, and solid, like mortar. "But they go fast. I just finished one and if I get one more I go home."

At that moment, Anne vowed to start reading romance novels also, especially the one with the sadly nude Fabio covers. She determined to carry them everywhere.

On the third day, she was called. The defendant, a young man, a child really, sat in an oversized suit coat. The judge explained the case: the man (child) was accused of fatally shooting another man.

Don't let me be called, Anne thought, though it made no sense now, since she had been called, and was in the midst of final jury selection, and a murder was involved. This was her nightmare and she did not know how to end such a thing, punch herself, maybe. If she didn't black out, the effect would cast serious doubts as to her mental state.

She wanted to put the helmet on and say, "Doctor's orders."

The judge asked people about their professions. One person said, "I'm a lawyer." She was kicked off right away.

Anne told all the things, and the people behind the things that they had forsaken her.

Anne said she was a teacher.

Then the judge wanted to know if anyone on the jury had ever been robbed.

Anne raised her hand. She did not look to see if anyone else had done so. She was too busy lecturing the wall for having abandoned her. But on the second question, "Anyone ever had trouble with a drug dealer?"

Now Ann was curious. She raised her hand and looked around. Her hand alone.

"Anyone ever have trouble with a police officer?"

Up shot her hand.

"Known an addict?"

Please, Anne thought. This is America. Who doesn't know an addict but the addict himself?

"How many times have you been robbed?" the judge

asked Anne, with suspicion. Anne explained the first, second, the third, the fourth, and the attempts, of course, which didn't count.

"Do you think these experiences will influence your judgment on this jury?"

How could Anne explain? The way she walked into the house, the way she locked the door, the way she triple-checked the locks once inside the door of her house, where she lived, why she taught, the way she breathed (count to ten inhale, count to ten exhale in any threatening situation, which was just about every situation) had been formed by her experiences. Every day she had to be the judge, but she never had to be jury, never had to condemn someone to a life sentence.

Anne nodded mildly: "I think so."

After a break, the judge said to Anne, "Both sides have agreed to let you go."

Anne couldn't remember what the judge said, after that: something about being sorry for those times.

The man (child) and a sheriff watched her leave.

Outside, she walked right up to where she'd locked her bicycle. She stood there, with a stare meant to bring the bike into her view. She thought maybe she had parked it in a different spot, so she walked around the dark hull where the building hung over the street, then asked the security guard on duty, who walked with her, and showed her how the expensive bikes had two locks, one horseshoe and one wire.

Her bike model had been discontinued. It was red, and smart, like the tricycle she had as a child. When Anne rode it around, often downtown, people admired its curvy frame.

But now, well, now the security guard said, "Is there a chance you locked it someplace else and forgot? Sometimes that happens."

Anne held her bike helmet as they walked around one corner, looking at people and across the road to the sign posts where other bikes were locked. They turned another corner. "Nothing there," the guard said, and then they turned another corner, and another, until they were not looking anymore, but simply walking around the block.

The security guard decided to offer a global perspective: "This happens all the time. You can buy the most expensive lock in the world, but if someone really wants your bike, they will find a way to get it."

She thought back to the judge's original question.

"These experiences have influenced me," she said.

The man didn't know what to make of such a comment.

"Hey don't blame yourself," he said.

She stared at the man's kind face.

"Okay."

She thanked him and left.

Anne walked home under a bold, wide sky. She was tired of holding the helmet, so she decided to put it on. She snapped the buckle closed. Someone walking by veered away from her. A woman did the same, then another, with a fear, then compassion.

Anne saw the universe and the objects. She saw the concern of passers by. She wanted to say consolingly, "It just feels good, like extra brain."

Instead, Anne saw the objects and the people behind the objects and felt an opening, where something broke free across her sky:

Life.

My life.

You have not forsaken me.

roby burns

maureen aitken

He the grandfather; she the granddaughter.

The last time they went to pick raspberries, he did not tell her to pull them gently, or look for the deep red color, or to notice the way they sagged like bumble bees from the weight of their time. She, as with every season before, had only to look his way and consider how his white, steady hands came in to coax the berry away from its own inevitable fall. He was tall, and wore a Scottish cap over his white hair. A black belt secured his blue pants, and under his clothes he wore pajamas, as did her other grandfather.

They had come to the raspberry field in his big blue car, a two-door, from the factory where he worked. She liked the boxy way of the car, and the smell, which was stale, but kind. With him she did not smoke or yell or get mad. She did not slam the door, as she would with her mother. The air was cool. And she had only to sit and watch. Her grandfather was quiet – that life had happened to him quiet. With him, she did not act.

It took some time to drive to the field, but she never had to make small talk. He listened to an AM radio program, the news usually, and they would drive along dirt roads where houses sat off far in the distance, and the fields surrounding them were green and roaming.

She did not ask him what it was like to breathe in coal dust at the mines, or what it was like in Terre Haute, or if he saw his brother-in-law die in the mine car accident. He did not ask her what she planned to do with her life, or if she was popular.

They picked in the morning, always the morning, when the berries were ripe and young and possible. She had a small basketful. He held his in the other hand, and peered into hers.

He said simply: "Good."

When they were done, they walked back to the car. He held the door open for her, and only when she put her seatbelt on, and her little bucket sat securely on the floor, did he close the heavy door softly.

He took her to a fast food restaurant. She did not know why. Maybe he preferred them, but she thought he might have done it for her, that he might have guessed it was something she had wanted. She knew not to ask, not because it would embarrass him, or that it was tactless. He was like the berries. You could not pull too much with this question or that question. He was very strong. But something in him, something as deep as the mines of his land, seemed perilously cracked. He had lived. And all his living was under safe keeping. You must not let it tear.

She got home that day, and her grandfather stayed for coffee. Her mother and grandfather talked of politics and finances and relatives. Sometimes, when he was listening, she saw how his lower lip hung down, how he stared at the floor.

Then, one time, in the midst if this concentration, he looked up at her, the granddaughter, and smiled proudly. His pajamas peeped out from under his shirt.

She smiled back. And soon he got up to leave, and she'd wished he would stay. She feared something new, something that might happen.

After he left, she took a cup, washed the little hairy berries and went upstairs with them. She used to put the hollow of the berries on her fingers, and pretend they were a pack of fancy ladies. It was not that way anymore.

She ate one dewy berry and tasted it and everything there, the earth, the sun, the water, and something else, something that took a long time that could not be named, but was good and true and long lasting. It was as if, in tasting this, a seed had been planted, a gift bequeathed, so it was not all too late.

She could not name it, but this moment, unknown, spoke to something bigger than The Depression, or destitution, or her own anger. Parents, two generations ago, had made sure it was hidden, tucked in the sun and earth of their son, where storms and winters were sure to come.

She thought not of accidents or trouble. No, she thought of his name, and of the colorful pajamas peeping out from under his shirt, and how all things turn to a sort of sleep that hopes for morning, and all parts of this world, from the coal mines to the burdened limbs, must know the weight of their time.

first fall

melanie richards

It was when I first fell in love that I began to confuse pleasure and pain: not at twenty-two or twenty-eight, but at thirty-seven, full-blown, divorced, my past life shattered into piles of refuse littering a random landscape.

I could see now the body's wisdom: how sex was an analog for something deeper, filling and emptying, threshing and sowing, the spaces created in our bodies by absence and desire. There was a hollow now where none had been before. Now my patient heart charted the interior and found a vast uninhabited stretch at the center, opening just under my solar plexus like the Great Plains rolling to the foot of the mountains. You were the mountains and everything stopped where you rose majestic and solitary, blocking an autumn sky now blue and still with longing.

It was enough sometimes just to say your name. Other times, nothing could satisfy me: voracious, I wanted to devour whole continents, songbirds in their gilded cages, myriad luminous small fish, the eyes of ghost cats prowling at midnight, the hands of clocks moving away and together, and the great beasts standing shaggy in their stalls. The world of appetite opened before me: oysters slid raw onto my tongue, I drowned golden raspberries in cream, roasted whole cloves of garlic in their papery skins, rolled and pounded raw dough and braided it and brushed it with butter and pressed in hazelnuts and citron and sprinkled on cinnamon and while the heat of the oven wooed it into being, I lay on the living room floor and breathed in its smell. In my herb garden, I crushed slender leaves of tarragon and feathery tendrils of fennel and I thought of your body, which I had not yet touched.

How do we bring a dream into being?
Slowly.

In that first garden, there was a man and a woman, a rib bone, hindsight and the hand of God. The trees bore down softly under their burden of fruit, apples always the wisest. Yet that story forgets the luscious marigold flesh of the apricot in its flushed velvety skin, something once private, now driven to open, ripe under the sky of paradise, heedless of death or wishes or any future but your name. It was this fruit I brought you, though I considered figs in their wrinkly green sacks, full of seed; or grapes, tumbling and dusky on the vines of heaven, bursting open on your tongue. I considered too the majestic melon, swelling, hollow, sweet fleshed and dripping; and the modest kiwis in their fuzzy jackets, those fruits we knew to plunder, slit open to show their startled, iridescent centers, like captured stars.

I wanted to lie with you in the billows of the new mown hay, in the sweet green smell of spring, and take the world and your body in my mouth.

I had been under a veil of ashes; grey was the bus in the afternoon traffic, gray its doors that shut and opened, gray its railings and its glass box full of coins. The things I'd learned had hurt and I resisted so each lesson was repeated two and even three times.

The women sat in rooms in the factories, the offices, and I sat with them. Desk after desk wedged in, inhospitable, and the steady clacking of the typewriter keys shut out the sound of birds. In the cities, they flew, dazed, straight into plate glass windows and broke their necks, their soft falling bodies accompanying us as we fell through the years.

It was easier before the longing, easier to fly fiercely right at the glass and, failing to break through, then easier, at least more final, just to fall and lie then on the concrete stunned and left for dead, perhaps prodded by a small boy with a stick on his way to some errand, whistling and bored, testing death with a branch or the toe of a torn sneaker.

I had fallen dazed into that world after divorce left my life undone, untidy, unraveling, everything I believed dissolving like Kleenex tissue in water.

And then you came.

So under this tree, on this night with stars tacked perilously to the black unconcern of the sky, lie with me. Lie down with me.

We can invent a heaven out of kindness, weaving a net of sleepless nights. We'll hang this net from the great lonely trees of paradise, resplendent with ripe bitten fruit, and when I touch you, the stars will blink out one by one and you will enter the sultry dark, climb over me, into me, again and again, while the wise blind birds fall backward into those burning nets.

squirt

nick healy

I was out behind the tool shed, just trying to sneak a smoke where no one would see, when Hunter, my dead brother's oldest, came around the corner and started in again.

"Uncle Pat, what are ya doin'?" He squinted in the sunshine and the skin on his red cheeks looked like it might crack. "You promised you'd let me drive the fishin' boat and now you're out here smokin' again. Is that all you're gonna do today?"

There were lots of things I'd like to have said right then, but most weren't the sort you say to your dead brother's boy, considering all the crap the kid's been through already and he's barely seven, especially considering he was there with your brother when some asshole in a Yukon lost control in an inch of snow, went ripping through the median, and smacked your brother's minivan—gashed into the driver's door and ripped him right out so when the kid looked for his dad all he saw was a hole and the world whizzing past.

What I could say, the nicest thing I could come up with, was, "Look, Hunter, I promised I would take you on the boat *today*, not *this morning*, not *this minute*."

Hunter stared back at me, his head tilted and mouth hanging open. He stood with his little legs squeezed together, said nothing, and kept on staring with that empty look kids have, like he'd been smacked on the forehead. I didn't know if I'd hurt his feelings or if he couldn't take a hint, but as long as he hung around, I didn't want to take another drag or even flip the ash into the soda can I'd brought along. Smoking in front of little kids always made me uncomfortable, and Hunter's mom used to bust my chops about it nonstop.

Hunter and I had a little standoff. I let the smoke rise and the ash grow. He watched it closely. We both kept quiet.

Then he broke. He started talking in his odd way, the last word of every sentence drawn out, almost like a little question, like he wasn't sure of anything. I watched his eyes, pinched by the brightness, and they stayed right on the cherry and the spent gray ashes hooking downward like a sickle blade. I didn't even know what he was going on about. I just watched him watching the cig waste away, and I couldn't stand it. I dropped the whole thing into the can and heard it fizz out.

"Are you done now? Can we get goin'?"

"Done?" I said. "I hardly got started. That was like throwing away twenty cents, you know that? Like taking two dimes and throwing them into the lake."

"You didn't have to put it out. I coulda waited. We coulda just talked."

Again, there was a huge difference between what I'd like to have said and what I could say to my dead brother's boy. I wanted to say, *Shit, kid, you're killing me. You're breaking my damn heart. I'm sorry I'm not a fun guy like your dad. I'm sorry I'd rather be alone*. But I couldn't say that.

"A nice offer," I said, "but your mother thinks I'm a bad example. She's probably right. So give me ten minutes, OK? Round up the life jackets, maybe a couple cans of Coke, and meet me at the dock."

Hunter smiled and sprinted off around the corner. He never walked anywhere; he always ran. Full speed.

I sat down in the grass, leaned back against the metal shed, hot from the morning sun, and smoked not one but two cigarettes all the way down to the filter. I smoked hard and fast. And I felt much better by the time I trotted down the hill in front of the cabin and out onto the dock.

Hunter sat in the bow of the fishing boat, facing backwards with his orange life jacket clipped on tight and two sodas on top of a crumpled beach towel at his feet. He smiled real wide when he saw me coming, and that made me feel good. While I untied the first line from the dock, he bent over and moved the Cokes aside. I threw off the second rope, climbed down into the boat, and sat down on the rear bench.

"You ready for some high-speed cruisin'?" I asked.

Hunter didn't say a word.

I looked up and found myself staring straight down the barrel of his new squirt gun, not one of those wimpy deals I had as a kid but one of these soaker things, where the kid pumps it up and lets fly. I sensed Hunter had done the pumping in advance. The enormous, shit-eating grin on his face gave that much away.

"Don't do it, Hunter," I said. "If you think I'm going to let you steer this—"

The stream went into my mouth like he was playing a carnival game, and when I closed my lips and turned my head, the water roared into my ear and drenched my hair, my cheek, my neck, my T-shirt. Hunter laughed until I leaned forward and jerked the gun out of his hands. I was too forceful and pulled him clear off his seat.

"You little snot," I said. "You're lucky I don't—"

Then I didn't know what to say. We froze like that, him wide-eyed with the metal edge of his bench pressed into his back and me holding a pink and yellow squirt gun and letting water drip from my face. What I wanted to say then was, *Why did you have to spoil this? You've been after me all morning, and you're about to get what you want. But you ruin it, ruin the whole damn day.* But pissed as I was, I couldn't say that.

I raised the barrel of the gun, pumped a couple times, and squeezed the trigger. A thin stream spurted onto Hunter's leg, then only air. He hooted and howled.

"Empty!" He laughed so hard that he couldn't speak.

I grabbed him under the armpits, lifted him high, and hurled his bony frame over the edge of the boat and into the lake. He spat and coughed when he came up, but he smiled and laughed between coughs. Then he whirled and swung one arm across the surface, sending a huge splash into the boat and onto me.

I didn't know what else to do, so I jumped in after him. In midair, I thought about the pack of cigarettes in my pocket, but it was too late to save them. When I caught up to Hunter, I lifted him high, put one hand under his tailbone, and launched him skyward the way I'd seen my brother do a hundred times on days just like this, like we'd never have again.

My brother's boy jackknifed into the water and came up wild-eyed and ready for more.

He screamed, "You're dead, Uncle Pat!"

His little legs churned until I let him catch me and drag me down. His fingernails gouged my skin as we rolled into the water, still clear and cold early in the season, and he wrapped his limbs around me. He clung hard to my back, but I found my balance, rose, and bucked him off. He crashed down, chopped in the water, and came up laughing again. We splashed and dunked each other until his mother came out of the house and hollered for us to stop.

hey you

pat cumbie

Before Johnson Street there was a boy I liked. Someone I even talked to. Not somebody made up, like Bill. This boy's name was Raul. We were living in this townhouse, which means that mother and I lived side by side with some other people. The boy I liked lived in a townhouse two doors down, all of their names written neatly on the mailbox in boxy letters. The townhouse we shared with some weird family, not students. We all lived at the edge of Madison, near Fitchburg. Apartments there were bigger and cheaper, townhouses, not funkified Victorians chopped into six pieces. Mother felt dangerously close to beige-land, but there was a swamp of sorts at the end of our street with standing water that had cattails and garbage in it. That made her feel better. The dad next door worked in a factory, graveyard shift, while the mom kept up with a toddler I nicknamed "hey you." That's all the kid would say and that's what his dad and mom called him all the time. We each had a stoop out front. That kid fell off it at least twice a day. First you'd hear him out there, "Hey you. Hey you. Hey you..." and then, "Wahhh!"

Mother said she thought the child was "under nurtured." He probably was a little neglected given that his name was Hey You, crawling around out there by himself like he did, but he seemed to have it OK. I'd found a crack in the wall in the basement between our place and theirs. Our side had mother's paintings and supplies. She used it as a studio. On their side they'd put down a carpet and some toys for him. He played down there a lot and seemed fine. In my opinion the only under nurtured person in the neighborhood was me. My mother never packed me a lunch or gave me an allowance.

Day after day I'd see Raul, and oh, man, he could make my heart go. He had black hair and dark eyes, and an unblemished tan. He was a little chubby, but I've never minded that. From a distance he seemed sweet, the way he stuck close to his older brother, or stood with his dad checking out the engine of their pickup, the way he helped his mother carry in groceries. It turned out he was just as nice up close, but it took me awhile to find out.

Before we spoke, he sent me a note. He left it visibly tucked and folded under the coffee can mother used to put her cigarette butts in. I found it on the stoop when I got home from school one day. He had sloppy boy handwriting. The note said "Dear Jacky, I think I like you. When read this meet me at the wamp. Raul M." He missed a few letters and spelled my name wrong, but when I read it, I felt as if he thought I was the only girl worth knowing. I held the note folded in my palm and carried it around clutched in my hand until it got damp. I became afraid my one and only love note would be ruined and put it in a shoebox on my dresser. It turned me into nothing but nerves, to meet him by the swamp, or anywhere else. So I stayed home, listening to a drizzle of "hey you" and ate microwave popcorn while mother paged through a book of paintings from the Middle Ages.

"Hey Jack, look at his," mother said. It was a series of pictures by a guy named Hans Memling. She called him a Flemish Primitive. They were about this saint named Ursula. The son of a king wanted to marry Ursula and she said "ok" but first she needed to go on a pilgrimage with 10,000 of her girlfriends to Rome. After three years they were on their way back to Germany when some Huns took them prisoner and murdered her and her companions. The whole series has this brave virgin point of view, especially at the last panel when Ursula's surrounded by all these guys at spearpoint.

A little white dog sits devotionally at Ursula's feet at the end. I enjoy that about some of the old paintings. There's always a loyal dog there. I couldn't see Babykins doing that for me but I told mother she needed to do a painting with Babykins even if he didn't deserve to be immortalized. Mother laughed and then told me the Ursula series was kept at a hospital in Brugge until it got its current home in a museum. Someday we'd have to go see it, she said. I don't want to see it, I told her. No way. Raul's note had made me feel a little sick and persecuted, like Ursula.

The next day on the bus Raul's brother asked me why I didn't go to the swamp. "I don't know," I told him. Facing how much I liked Raul and wanting to meet him was like going to witness a saint's butchering. I just couldn't do it. He pointed toward Raul at the back of the bus. "That boy loves you. Give him a chance." I looked at Raul and felt terrible. He *loves* me? Love and hope seemed to prompt Raul into shrugging his shoulders, as if to prove he was harmless. His brother was intent on matchmaking. "You can meet him after school."

Mother didn't know if Ursula actually liked the king's son, but probably not if she was gone three years. I did like Raul, but I didn't like having to do something about it.

Eventually we did start up a friendship. Raul was a very likeable person. The thing I liked about him most was that he was polite, not at all pushy like his brother. If he truly loved me, he kept it to himself, which I appreciated. Instead he talked about all the interesting things his mother fixed for dinner, like tamales and chilaquiles, and once he brought me some sweet-sour home made Kool-Aid type drink made with something called hibiscus. It was good.

In return I showed him mother's artwork in the basement. He pretended to like her work, and I pretended not to feel sorry for him. He had no idea what he was getting into down there. Fitchburg inspired my mother to do these mud-colored abstractions that had meticulously painted saints painted on them—they were either praying and looking pious or getting x-rayed by God (who must be hidden in the clouds) in an annunciation type fashion. The saints looked like the people who worked at the 7-11 where our street met the highway. Mother went whole hog with the two dimensional Medieval look for the characters, with the goldleaf, the deep reds and blues. It occurs to me now that maybe mother's paintings might of freaked him out. Seeing his own mother's saints and Madonnas manipulated that way by the likes of my mother might have been too much.

We talked a little about how we hated Fitchburg. He told me he didn't like having to be Mexican here. I told him I didn't like to have to ride the bus. Once I said it I knew our beefs weren't even close to equal. I got the feeling that he might not love me anymore.

Mother told me shortly after that we were moving again. I thought maybe it was for the best this time. I went to tell Raul and we sat together on his stoop. He told me that there was something he needed to tell me too. Something he should've told me right away. Raul told me that his name wasn't pronounced like rawl, it was rah-ool. Rah. Ool. I rolled his name through my mouth, puckering up on the ool part. I was practicing rah-ool, over and over, just like the little neighbor boy, hey you hey you hey you, and Raul leaned over and kissed my pursed lips.

so this is

patricia zontelli

Night moves nearer to the window. There is something on the radio. At last warning, the lanterns are lit. The three of them – the girl, her grandparents – must leave.

The old man is confused; he keeps asking how old he is. His wife, having nothing else, chews on an onion. The young girl with rings under her eyes wishes it were time to go home to her parents, for supper. She has her own way of watching. One thing she knows is that she needs plenty of room to walk around.

The boats are loaded. The old woman refuses to shut the door; she cannot come down from herself. She is swamped by memories - leaving is so difficult. The old man is enveloped in mist; he is backwards walking along a foggy beach with his dog that, when it whined, sounded like music reversed, rising back up to a mouth.

There is this maneuvering now; the ship's anchor is

dragging along ocean's floor. They've arrived.

The girl says *So this is America.* The old woman counts her coins again, places them in her sleeve for safety. The old man eyes his suitcase, whatever he can listen for. He has forgotten his name. His wife keeps it for him in her apron pocket.

***

The girl, Klara, says nothing, keeps her hands deep down in her coat pockets. Breathing the unfamiliar, crowded among the unwashed, raggedy bodies of other disembarking passengers, she is relieved to have made it out of the airless hold of the ship. The weather is fierce; she pulls her woolen headscarf down over her face. Wind roars and heavy wet snow falls and falls on the roof of the building they are entering. It is huge, wooden with a peaked roof, like a ship upside down in a storm. The room even smells of ship: mold, vomit, shit.

It's as crowded and sour in here as it was on the crossing, but now, everyone is whispering or silent, as if holding their breath. Mothers hush the cries of their children—some curl the ends of their neck scarves, stuff them in their baby's mouths. Grandmother smoothes a hand over Grandfather's back to comfort him, a finger to her lips as she shushes, shaking her head at Klara, who is pressing her lips together so tightly they are beginning to quiver.

"Cannot think… I forget..," said Grandfather, rubbing his forehead. *"What is my name?"* he hisses to Grandmother, tugging her coat sleeve.

"Shh," said Grandmother. "We must be quiet. And careful."

Queues of people move like larvae in crooked lines leading to green tables. A lantern suspends over a man seated at each, wearing a flat hat and scribbling, dipping his pen over and over into a bottle of ink. Uniformed men, hands behind their backs, mill behind those seated. None of them are smiling. Klara notices that one of the uniforms is worn by a woman. She has tiny golden earrings like her mother's.

***

She wishes her grandparents would move faster; they're never quick enough. All three of them are round and waddling, carrying on their bodies all possible clothes. Klara has given up scratching the itch at the back of her neck where the wool sweaters chaff; it just makes her want to scratch more. The three of them smell like each other now.

It's taken hours for them to reach the head of the line; Klara has fallen asleep leaning against her grandmother's back and is startled when Grandmother suddenly moves forward to the table, breathing heavily, dragging her brown cardboard suitcase over the stone floor, making a loud *scritch;* the eyes of the woman with the earrings warn them from across the room

Grandmother supports her husband by the crook of his arm, holds him upright. He's drooling; his spittle against his black suit coat looks like the shiny trail of a snail. She does the talking. The man in the flat cap doesn't understand even one word. His hand holding the pen over the inkbottle begins to shake and jump, dripping small black dots over their passports.

Klara wishes she could tell the serious man puzzled by their papers that if they do not want her in their country, she would be happy to go back. In fact, she would give them everything she owns to do so: the watch and chain they took from her father's pocket when they found him in the forest, her mother's tiny mirror they'd held to her mouth before the white sheet settled - before she became a landscape of a mother under the cloth: her breasts a mountain, her small nose a hill, her long black hair a waterfall tumbling out from under the sheet, over the edge of the mattress.

Klara knows their family dog, Mucha, is waiting for her—he will wait forever on the doorstep of their house at the edge of the village. She imagines snow falling on the house, on Mucha; his head is back and he is moving his mouth in a way that looks like he is calling *Klara!* although no sound comes out.

***

It is for him that Klara needs to return.

She sits on her grandmother's suitcase waiting for the doctors to finish examining her grandfather behind a white cloth screen, thinks of huddling down with her dog under straw, their breath mingling in the air, darkness a blanket all around; stars above; owls, with their wide eyes, watching. Mucha licks the inside of her arm, her face. She can almost feel the wetness.

She falls into a dream of matches, striking *whick! whick!* match after match on the stone floor to light the tin lanterns, the *hump, hump* of the ship. She dreams of Tomas leaning against a mirror, his open mouth drooling, steaming glass. Water sloshes against a porthole. All the faces foreign, sharp. The bearded man telling get ready for anything. On deck, a breeze the size of a small arm lifts her grandfather's white hair; his back turned, he stares over the water to his dog, singing. Her grandmother puts her strong arms around his shoulders, holds him tight.

When Klara returns to her village, she and Mucha will live in the forest behind her house. She will build a shelter of pine boughs and mud, she will catch fish in the creek to feed them, find roots. *I will not eat even as much as a tiny child,* she promises herself. *There will be enough.* Yes.

divorce

patrick hueller

The wind was blowing and had got the lake going. White caps splashed against the dock. The girl was not a girl at all anymore but thirteen, an adolescent, and she was bobbing in the lake, way out there, not a speck but far enough away to look pretty small, and for the water to be pretty deep. Her life jacket lay on the dock, where her mother was standing. Her mother was screaming to her. *Get back here!* she was screaming. *Get back here this second, young lady!* The dad was there, too, but he was yelling at the mother. *Let her be,* he was yelling. *What's the worst that can happen?* The wind was picking up; in a few minutes the rain would start. And the thunder. *Get back here!* the mother screamed. *Get back here this instant! Let her be,* the dad yelled. *Just let her be.* The girl was bobbing, bobbing, kicking below the water's surface.

end zone

patrick hueller

My twin brother is on his knees. "Hut!" he calls, and looks to his left. We're in the backyard, playing football: me, my sis, and my two brothers. My twin recently had surgery on both feet—a solution to a congenital problem, we hope. Bones were removed. So, he's playing on his knees. All-time quarterback. We've been out here a while now, and we've been taking it easy on him; letting him get off his passes, letting the intended receiver catch them. But now he's getting cocky. He's talking trash. He's on fire, he's telling us; he can't miss. He can't believe we can't stop this aerial assault of his, this bombardment of leather missiles. He won't shut up. So this time, as he watches our sister begin her slant route, my brother and I decide to clamp down on the defense. We double team her. We hold her and grab her and we won't let her get free. All the time we're looking back at my twin brother, waiting to step in and intercept his throw. But it turns out he's not throwing; he's tucking the ball under his arm and running for the end zone. Or, crawling for it, I mean. The end zone, which is the edge of the yard, is a full twenty yards away, and he's trying to crawl every yard of it. It's ludicrous—and I can't let him get away with it. I can't be like those parents who let their kids win at everything, like those dads who pretend to huff and puff after racing their seven-year-old. I let go of my sister, run after the ball carrier. Close in fast. He sees me coming, tries to accelerate, but it's no use. I lower my shoulder, brace for the impact.

available for an epiphany

ray gonzalez

The longest word used by Shakespeare in any of his works is "honorificabilitudinitatibus." Believe me when I say it doesn't mean the lone black hair that sticks out of your big right toe just below the toenail. The word for that hair is slypadorelystybold. Pregnant goldfish are called "twits," but my father used to call me a dummy, a goof-ball, like those stinking moth balls in closets that held his four pair of golf shoes whose spikes dug into the closet carpet, a detail only I can remember because my slarapin is alive. In other words, my second heart—that one that resides inside my soul and beats for the past and is able to put these things together. Graffito is the little-used singular of the much used plural word graffiti, but manes is not the plural for more than one moon because to mistake mane for moon would mean I could not rise in the middle of the night, suffering from insomnia, and be able to go write something about a moon I have not seen in months, my words glowing on my computer screen brighter than the graffito I thought I dreamed about when I heard a friend of one of my nephews had been gunned down in a drive-by. Narcissism is the psychiatric term for self-love as in the lone artist compelled to ignore his masterpiece leaning on the canvas because the cracked mirror in his tiny apartment is showing him too many stark visions he has not been able to conjure up through the powerful fumes rising out of the dozens of tubes of oil paints that are squashed all over the floor. A language becomes extinct in this world every two weeks. A silence fills the halls every three months, its source a secret, its ability to envelop and slow down the development of rapture a completely natural and potent thing that is best avoided from dusk to dawn, though one vital moment appears on the border of light and darkness as if something is about to touch those of us who have even the slightest clue as to what is going on. In 1961, Italian artist Piero Manzoni packed his feces in cans, signed and mounted them, and then sold them as art. This story about the natural elements of man is a very common one, an epic no artist or writer is able to comprehend because the canned stuff is the purest form of artistic expression, the fact it is imprisoned in a container an excellent metaphor about creative souls who will create anything in order to get from here to there without having to step on too much shit, without having to face the crap in their lives or acknowledge what their mighty and private visions are truly made of. Old story, open the can. In 1983, a Japanese artist, Tadahiko Ogawa, made a copy of the Mona Lisa completely out of ordinary toast. Well, there was a football player for the New York Giants with the nickname "Toast" because he was burned all the time for touchdowns. So, what? Toast. Crossing one's fingers is a way of secretly making the sign of the Cross. It was started by early Christians to ask for divine assistance without attracting the attention of pagans. Crossing the toes is a way of secretly making sure you are still alive, the rare ability to actually cross your toes saying more than I can possibly say. A baby octopus is about the size of a flea when it is born. I once saw a flea the size of an octopus, but it was dead. A slug has four noses. My memories have only one nose. 62 degrees Fahrenheit is the minimum temperature required for a grasshopper to be able to hop. I have a brass statue of a grasshopper in my office, but it doesn't do me any good because the wise man called me once and said, "Grasshopper," and the awful world showed up instead. Fine-grained volcanic ash can be found as an ingredient in some toothpaste. So can blood. Some asteroids have other asteroids orbiting them. Some hemorrhoids have other hemorrhoids orbiting around them. Devoid of its cells and proteins, human blood has the same general makeup as sea water. I prefer the river.

jackknife

ronald wallace

He thought she didn't love him anymore. Relations between them had been strained, to say the least. As they sat there at the picnic table at their farmhouse in Prairie County, Wisconsin, the weedy box elders and dead or dying elms stretching off in the gully like a broken promise, a mockingbird twirping merrily on a fence post, he wondered.

Their ten-year-old daughter, Phoebe, oblivious to the tension in the air, was twirping merrily, too, something about lost jackknives and miraculous recoveries. "Isn't that amazing?" she twittered, flapping her small arms and levitating a good three feet above the table.

"Slow down," he said, though he knew she was just frantically happy they were all back together. He gazed across the gully at the hillside glistening with the first rain in weeks, the oak trees dim and shimmering under the broken clouds. "Listen," he said. "Here's a story about a jackknife--a true story. When I was a kid, about your age, Phoebe, my father took me fishing in Minnesota. The first day out I accidentally dropped his favorite jackknife over the side of the boat. We were fishing the deep water for Northerns, and, though he solemnly proposed lowering me down on a line to retrieve it, it was lost. Two days later, I caught the biggest Northern I'd ever seen--must have been ten pounds. When my father cut it open . . ."

"Oh, come on," his wife began, but he talked over her.

"When he cut that Northern open in the fish house late that night—this is a *true* story—*the pearl-handled jackknife wasn't there!* No. That jackknife was lost. We never found it."

There was a moment of silence. The sun had set behind the black clouds in the hollow, and the spring peepers had begun their tremulous warbling in old man Goff's horse pond. And then his wife was laughing, and his daughter too, their voices like bright goldfinches high on the wires, or tiny bells swelling in the distance, ringing from runnel to rivulet, the whole valley lit like a crystal glass of milk, spring peepers coupling in the lush romantic dusk.

why my left leg is longer

shana youngdahl

My sister Juliet busily scattered hands around the yard. She collected and dissected dolls by the dozens. She used the parts for art projects that gradually filled up our two acres. Until last September, our parents allowed her to do artwork in the house. Then Dad came home and found her frying up a pan of Barbies. "Damn it Juliet! That shit's not good to breathe!" he pushed her from the stove and turned on the fan. "Go outside and find your sister!" He leaned into the windows and cranked each one open. Juliet mumbled something about how Eva Hesse worked with all different kinds of plastics, and how dare he stifle her artistic urges. I tried not to laugh, not because of her fourteen year-old tirade but because I successfully hid right under their noses.

I am small enough to fit inside many of our kitchen cabinets. I hid in them almost as soon as I learned to open them, and nobody ever looked for me there. The big one under the sink is my favorite because it smells like the soap on Mom's hands and is full of empty vases, onions, potatoes and bright orange scrubbies. The only problem is when I surprise someone in the kitchen by accidentally kicking the bin of sweet potatoes. When one rolls out the door and onto the floor I nearly have to stop breathing in order to avoid detection by a hand reaching in to replace the stray tuber.

The day Juliet scattered hands in the yard was like most others, sunny, seventy degrees with a light breeze. Our parents were out and we were supposed to be alphabetizing our bookshelves but I spent most of the morning trying to figure out if it was really possible for a kid my size to climb inside the chimney. The night before, Dad read us William Blake at bedtime and Juliet didn't believe that kids my age ever worked, or died inside chimneys like the rats in our walls. I wasn't worried about dying because we rarely use our chimney. Our mother is afraid of everything which might pose a danger of fire, and she has the chimney swept after every use. Mom is more than paranoid about fire, she has a small library of fire facts in the living room which we are expected to read from weekly. We each have a fire-proof safe in or bedroom. "Not that we own anything of monetary value but you wouldn't want to have to replace everything would you?" She says each year when we select our one outfit to be locked away in our safe. "It is important to have something of your own. No matter what happens, you know how it is in California, drop a match and the whole state could disappear."

It took only seconds for me to scurry six feet up chimney, my body pressed between cool stone and bumps of cement patching. I sneezed, and I kept sneezing. A little square of blue light criss-crossed with birds suddenly didn't seem like an appealing destination. I thought I could exhale and slide on my toes down to the living room. I exhaled. I exhaled and lifted my toes. I did not slide. A shadow passed over the blue square above me. I became aware of each ridge in the stone supporting my back. I tried to yell for Juliet, but I couldn't turn my head down. I started spitting. I thought if I could spit enough I could grease myself out of the chimney and not end up like a smothered rat.

When I was younger I got my head stuck between the bunk bed and the wall. I remember everything was upside down and how the bumps on the ceiling looked like Sesame Street characters. The chimney didn't offer that kind of entertainment. Everything was black. The stone pulled at my body's heat. I spit until my mouth was dry and I still didn't slide towards the living room. I focused my eyes on the blue and tried to count the birds.

I awaited my death.

The cat peeked in on me first. I heard her feeble meow and I talked to her. "Robot, kitty, kitty, go tell them I am stuck up here! Come on Robot!" Robot swished her tail, meowed and disappeared. When the sun was directly above the blue square I knew my sister would be coming inside for food. I tried to make as much racket as possible but the stone absorbed by noises. Then I heard something crinkling and the strike of a match. Juliet lit something beneath me.

"Juliet!" I screamed.

"Holy Mother of God!" She shouted. I heard her beating out whatever she had ignited below me. "Boo, what are you doing up there?"

"I wanted to find the fifty-seventh way to climb onto the roof," I lied.

"Didn't make it did you?"

"Nope."

"Okay, hold on, I am going to pull you down." Juliet reached in with one arm and tugged my left leg. I felt some skin rip off my cheek. I pressed my feet into the wall to try and slow the fall, and I caught again but Juliet yanked my leg harder.

"You trying to pull my leg off?" I winced.

"Well, I hadn't thought about that," Juliet laughed as I slid down. My feet rested in the half-ash of her paper doll collection.

"Lucky for you I decided to burn something."

"Uh-huh." I felt dizzy. I gasped for fresh air.

"You're bleeding all over," she said handing me a green doll dress to clean myself. "Give it back when you're done. It's not often I get to use real blood."

I held the dress to my bleeding face and examined the scrapes on my knees. Juliet left the living room and came back with a bottle of peroxide. She instructed me to lean into the fireplace and close my eyes when she poured half the bottle over my face.

"Damn Boo. How'd you get so stoic? Your face is bubbling off and you don't even make a noise?"

"Dunno," I said.

"You're a doggone trooper little one."

"Uh-huh," I muttered. She put her hands on my chin. They smelled like plastic and tempura paint.

"And too big to be tunneling all over the house like a go-per," I smiled. Gopher was my first word. As an infant I shouted "Gopher" when Juliet crawled under the sheets of our parent's bed. Her body plowed up the blankets, just like the dirt trails in our parents' garden.

"Juliet," I hesitated.

"Yeah?"

"I guess we should alphabetize the books before they get home." I shuddered at the suggestion. She probably had several projects to do—maybe she was going to finish the birdbath of doll torsos she'd been working on for weeks.

"Yeah, we should," she said, standing and reaching to help me up. When I stood I could feel it, the slight change in my leg's shape, half of myself slightly taller, and the rest, just waiting.

swimming lessons

sigrid tornquist

Thea took it all in, "in" boys, "in" girls, "in" clothes, circled up as if for protection, snickering. They took turns stealing not-so-subtle glances at the backpack-toting, myopic, victim of the day, unwittingly sporting the word "LOSER" taped to his back. She took two quick steps to catch up to him, bumping him just enough to dislodge the sign. "Sorry," she mumbled.

"It's OK," he smiled. So unaware.

In unison they flipped her the bird.

First bell rang and instead of entering, as she should, she turned and ran. She ran with a heavy rhythm as if pressing herself into the sidewalk, turning every so often to look behind her. Dark circles appeared under her arms as drops of sweat trailed into her eyes. She slowed to a walk as she descended the hill, counting the cars she could see in the parking lot. Three today. Not a lot. The pink Caddy was there. Always the pink Caddy. She wondered what brought him here to sleep in his car, by the river. The other two cars, black and shining in the morning sun, parked side by side. Middle-aged men sitting behind their steering wheels, waiting. Her friends thought it was weird. Hanging out by the river alone. "All sorts of creepy things go on down there, you know." Maybe. Maybe just people alone. Maybe just lonely people.

She made her way through the underbrush, shoes filing with sand. She must not have run fast enough. Anger caught up with her. She was sick of cardboard cut-out people unacquainted with the word "depth." Of trying to find the right thing to wear. The right thing to say. The right group to disappear in. She shook her head and walked faster. As she neared the edge of the river she stopped. There, back turned toward her, stood an old man. Maybe 60. God, even older than her parents. His hands reached high up toward the sun, then out to each side, down to his toes and rested on his hips. He twisted right, left, and right again. He wore red shorts that fell just above his knees and on his feet were mismatched flip-flops.

He grabbed the edge of his faded tee shirt and pulled it over his head, exposing alarmingly blue-white sagging skin. He folded the shirt once in half, rolled it up and set it under the oak, roots exposed yet still budding life. He kicked off his flip-flops and waded out into the rush of water, leaned forward and began to swim. His strokes were strong and confident as he let the current carry him downriver. Thea stood there, hypnotized. Crazy old man.

The next day she dispensed with the pretense of stopping by school and headed back to the river. He was there. She hid herself behind the trees and watched him stretch and twist, methodically undress and swim. Today the backstroke.

Day after day it was the same. Sometimes backstroke. Sometimes front. She loved watching his practiced movements executed with grace and purpose. She envied him. On the day that she should have been taking her SATs she stood, barely visible, behind the branches of a low-hanging tree. After his swim, he walked past her hiding place, turned his head slightly, and said, "I know you watch me."

"I…uh…," she stammered, but he kept walking, uninterested in her response.

So…she watched him. Sometimes he would comment as he passed, looking straight ahead without slowing his pace.

"Still hiding, I see." "Face it." Things like that.

Only once did she venture to say something. "I'd be scared," she whispered. "Swimming the river alone."

This time he stopped. Turned fully to face her. "I'm more scared not to," he said.

The next morning he swam without audience. Thea stood fidgeting in the great double doorway and readied herself to lean into her own particular current.

bomb threat

sue taylor

My desk is scooted into the darkest part of the Quonset hut, so that I can read *Burro on the Beach* while Mrs. Richards makes everybody else go through the math assignment. I hate math, especially fractions. I just can't do it, and if I stay in the back and don't make any noise, she'll leave me alone and I won't have to. Another acoustic tile falls from the ceiling and hits Zach Hughes, which is good, because he's a dick. They must be testing out at the range. The ceiling's been falling all day.

I go back to *Burro on the Beach,* hidden in my math book. The kids in the book are on the beach with their burro, making s'mores. I wish I had a burro. I wish I lived at the beach instead of in the desert. I look up in time to see Mrs. Richards grab one of the Tiffany's shoulders. She's bending over, checking her work. I open my desk and flump the book into all the stuff inside. I get a lot of demerits because of my desk. I feel around and find my big table of soft paper with solid pale blue lines and a dotted blue line between them—if I look busy, Mrs. Richards will leave me alone. There's a knock on our classroom door, and then Mrs. Richards is making us form our usual single file line and march out of the room. We march to the farthest edge of the playground and then she tells us it's a bomb threat, and that we will stand there until the base bomb squad authorizes reentry to the school. I look over and the big kids from the junior high annex are standing around on the other side of the playground. We watch the bomb squad go from building to building. No building explodes and they don't bring any bombs out, and then it's 3:00, the busses come, and we can go home.

That week, there are three more bomb threats. Mrs. Richards sighs and leads us all out of the classroom a little more slowly each time. In Assembly, we get a lecture from the man who usually comes once a year to tell us not to talk to people who ask us what our parents do. He tells us we will go to jail if we make bomb threats. The microphone squeals and he thumps it with his finger. Then he tells us that they think they know who is doing it. And. The. F.B.I. Is. Investigating. Everybody gets quiet after that. The man looks out at us, and I look down at my hands when his eyes move toward me. Even though it's not me doing it, I feel like it is. I like the bomb threats and every day I'm in school I hope for one.

Although I never stop hoping, there are no more bomb threats the rest of elementary school or junior high.

There haven't been any bomb threats since I started high school, but high school is interesting on its own. Sitting on a rock out in the desert, drinking a Dr. Pepper with a mix of liquors carefully stolen from my parents' liquor cabinet, each bottle left at the same relative level, I find out who the Bomber was.

"You're kidding," I say to Michael van Dreisen, the most straight-edge person I know, "You?"

"Yeah, Beth, me," he says, frowning at my drink. He doesn't experiment with alcohol, as he puts it. He's so well-adjusted and mature that the only thing he does wrong is hang out with me in the desert at night.

I sit on the rock, staring into my Dr. Pepper. Except for really believing that building better missiles will lead to world peace, Michael's the most normal person in the world. He's a National Merit Scholar. He lettered in track and swimming. He's on the Forensics team and he's a Mathlete. He actually has fun at the pep rallies. Not only all that, but his father is on the base bomb detection and removal squad.

"No way that was you," I tell him. He folds his arms and looks me in the eyes.

Years later, after dropping out of college again, I get a

letter with no return address on the envelope. It's from Michael, enclosing my Social Security card, which he found under the seat of his car. I must have lost it there the last time we both were home for Christmas, about three years ago. The letter wants to know if I've been feeling socially insecure since then, and includes a phone number with a 619 prefix. Our hometown is 619, so I decide he must be living there despite all the vows not to be one of the people who end up going back. A slow job in the defense industry and a big, cheap house in Ridgecrest is the La Brea Tar Pits for human beings. I call the number and let it ring for a while, waiting for a machine to pick up, and he answers the phone in a whisper.

"What's up?" I ask, after he informs me that San Diego is also in the 619 area code. He tells me, very quietly, that a few nights ago something ripped open and partially ate a bag of grits he had sitting on the kitchen counter. He suspects a rat is climbing up the palm tree by his kitchen window, coming in and eating his grits. He is sitting in the dark at the kitchen table with a bottle of whiskey and a loaded Sig Sauer .380. I ask what he's using as a bullet stop.

"The rat," he whispers.

"Seriously," I say, "if you shoot at this grits-thieving rat, won't the bullet go through the wall and maybe hit somebody?"

"No," he tells me, "I'm using the same bullets the Israelis use for hijackers."

"Oh," I say "huh." I hear the shugging gurgle of a bottle being inverted, and a soft swallowing noise.

"Excuse me," he says.

"Certainly," I say. After that, there's a moment when neither of us says anything, and then I ask: why not try trapping the rats? He has, he says, and the traps didn't work. The rats are too smart. So, I ask him, why not just shut your window?

"Too hot for that," he says.

Keep the grits in a rat-proof container?

"The bag's too big," he says.

"Okay," I say, so you get this rat. Won't there be others?"

"Let 'em come," he says, "I have a lot of bullets."

I look out my own kitchen window. There's a full moon. I picture it above Michael's apartment building in San Diego. Silver-blue light streams in through the window he's left open for the rat, one ray stretching out to make the whiskey on the table glow. I see the moonlight illuminating his profile, glazing the hand nearest the gun.

"If any reporters ask me about you," I say, "I'll just tell them you were a quiet, polite young man."

"Do that," he says.

isolette

sun yung shin

1. I reached into the isolette and turned the baby on its side, gently but firmly like turning a breakfast sausage link, as to keep the browning even on all sides.

2. The baby did not protest, but it did turn its twin black eyes at me and blink, like the animal it was. I blinked back. I felt something tender pulse to life within me. It was as though a little glass opened up a space in time, a little circle of memory, a little round of moonlight. Old-fashioned Korean combs are round, or at least I think they are, and I longed to hold one in my palm, its even teeth making a series of small red dots, a temporary score.

3. There was a visitor, a priest, or a cleric of some sort. Unfortunately, he smelled dank and old. The skin on his cheeks was mottled like a toad, and somehow shiny as though worn down, down, down. There was hair in

his ears and it was black, but his eyebrows were white. He looked like some kind of forest animal, I glanced at his greasy black cuffs and half expected to see broken branches and rusty leaves issuing forth, competing for space with his bony yellow wrists.

4. We talked about clouds, about how they were simultaneously worldly and ethereal, an illusion, heaven made of water droplets and dust particles. How we saw our futures and our pasts in them, but never our present. He said, "The term I use for cloud's appeal is *eidetic charisma*." At this utterance, the baby blinked, twice, and began to cry. Its toothless, dark mouth was the size of my question and just as unanswerable.

5. "I love that term. Here, let me write that down," I reached for a plain ball point pen, its end chewed to wet feathers, and a sheet of lined paper. *EIDECTIT—*

"No, that's not it! You're missing a C, and you have an extra T"

EIDETICT—

"No! You're not listening!"

"You, spell it for me again, slowly—"

"E – I – D..."

As I wrote down the letters they began to change. When I looked down at the paper again, they had multiplied, and rearranged themselves into something like this:

CARNEAFORM ANDELENTEARNICON DEAQUISTICONUIS

I tried to write again and long drops of black ink splashed onto the paper. I shook the pen, hard. On the page, shapes began to form. Clouds, no horses. Four spotted horses, running. I looked up at the priest, or the cleric. The baby had stopped crying and was chewing a corner of its blanket.

6. I noticed that the blanket, a cheap affair more like a cotton kitchen towel than a blanket, was printed with pastel hot air balloons. This same blanket, or its copy, or its cousin, was the same that the American hospitals wrapped around my own children after their births, washings, weightings, and scorings. I thought then, as

I did here, that hot air balloons were a poor choice for something so newly subject to the laws of gravity, and ordinary oxygen, and falling.

7. The man was gone. I turned the baby on its back, to look at the crack in the ceiling, and I ran after him.

8. There is more to the dream, but it involves the odor of smoke, and tiny white worms swimming through the carpet at the orphanage, or the primary school. It involves children upturning their plastic lunch trays and a nun, the receptionist, shaking in anger.

9. I went back to the baby, of course.

10. Her eyes were dry, and bright, and she didn't seem to mind the irony of the hot air balloons on her towel-blanket. Her forehead seemed to show no memory of the priest-cleric, no troubles creased her little yellow-pink brow. She had a little constellation of milia on her nose, that was all. I put my little finger into her hand and she grabbed it, and held on tight.

11. The Korean orphanage worker swept by and said something in Korean that sounded like a question. I no-

ticed her slim ankles and flat black shoes. They left no footprints on the hard white floor. My own shoes were chunky and seemed foreign, though they were made in China.

12. I leaned down to the baby and I had the urge to bite her, but instead I gave her the smallest kiss. I combed her tuft of black hair with my fingers and pinched her tiny ear, just a little edible mushroom, and left my mark, if only for a moment.

13. The sound of horses or the odor of clouds—

angel's eye

suzanne nielsen

Angel Olson's nerves graze the top of her bumpy pink skin like Mendel's law mementos. Behind her thick glasses, the bumps grow to the size of mosquito bites, reminding me of Pacman icons ready to munch, or of a neighborhood of round people. Maybe I notice those eyelids more because Angel doesn't have eyelashes or eyebrows. Angel sits across from me in tenth grade art class at a table that looks similar to the one in the painting of Christ's last supper. She draws the same picture from one day to the next, changing only the shading. It's always an eye, the right, with a tear falling from the corner. I can't tell whose eye she draws; she only draws with pencil and never adds color. Angel talks all the time, but under her breath. I can't tell what she's saying and for weeks I don't interrupt.

Today in class our substitute teacher says we are supposed to draw the person across from us with colored chalk. I ask Angel if she wants to comb her hair before I start. I ask her if my hair looks okay, fluffing up the front, I ask if I need to reapply lipstick or blush. I'm feeling like I have to puke, but I want to look my best. She mumbles something under her breath and I decide to let it go. "Okay," I say, "do you want to take your glasses off so I can see your features better?" Angel says, although barely audible, "When you draw, you start with the inside of a person, not their appearance." That sounds to me like she's been spending too much time in Mr. Ellis's psychology class or in Ms. Mitchell's cooking class with microwaves. But in a way I'm impressed. She appears deep; maybe there's more to Angel than I think.

As Angel and I sit drawing, I ask what it's like living with Larry Wilhelme, the cutest boy in school. Angel's a foster kid, living with Wilhelmes on the corner of Frost and Johnson Parkway, right across the street from me. "He's an asshole," Angel says in a whisper. Wilhelmes have 13 kids of their own, 12 of them ordinary, and one, Larry, who is every girl in Johnson High School's fantasy boyfriend. "He's an asshole on the ice," I say. "But then again, we need him to be if we're to go to state for the tournament." Larry is the goalie for our school's hockey team, and his appearance is often enhanced with a black eye. His nose forms an "L" from being broken so many times, but I love that because my name, Lydia, starts with the same letter. I'm convinced Larry's nose is representative of my name, even if he doesn't know it yet. Needless to say, I'm not opposed to Angel's whimsical way of thinking. "But getting back to what you said earlier," I say, "I couldn't agree with you more. It's what's inside a person," I say, '"that makes him or her beautiful." Angel glares at me with those magnified bumpy eyelids. Her chalk is talking louder than she is. "Larry's an asshole inside," she says, still under her breath, then adds, "and his old man's no better."

Mr. Wilhelme supports his family by taking in foster kids and selling jewelry he finds with his metal detector. Mrs. Wilhelme never sits down, except late at night, I sometimes see her on her porch year round smoking a cigar. Mrs. Wilhelme wears a pentagon symbol made out of nickel around her neck on a black rope. It swings in unison to her to-and-fro motion of her huge breasts. She always has on the same dress whether it's summer or winter. Every season its yellow fades to a more solid consistency of beige. The same color I'm using to outline Angel's face on my chalk portrait. I search for color variation, give her hair a livelier color than the one I'm using for her outline, although in real life her hair and skin tone match. "Here's the perfect color," I say as I hold up a color called Vanilla Vogue. "Is my talking making it difficult for you to draw me?" I ask Angel. She says, "Talk away," then smiles. Her teeth are also the color of Vanilla Vogue, but I won't make this portrait that representative of her. I won't put in the red bumps on her eyelids and I'll draw in lashes and brows. I'll make Angel into a homecoming queen, sunken cheeks, and beautiful squared chin with a dimple. Even a trace of glow in her otherwise murky irises.

"Did you see Larry play his heart out last night?" I ask Angel. "I hate hockey," she says. How could anyone possibly hate hockey, I think. "Well, the sport isn't for the faint hearted," I say as I search for a cinnamon shade for Angel's eyebrows. My drawing of Angel isn't the best. I've never been a serious art student but I've watched caricaturists at the fair work their magic. They always start with the eyebrows. But then again, they usually have a model with brows to work with.

"You ever see a baby born dead?" says Angel, staring at me with bald eyes. I grab hold of my stomach and squeeze it. "It's not for the faint hearted," she adds. I wonder if Angel is a witch or in conspiracy with the devil. Talking like this, those weird bumps on her lids. Her catatonic coloring. "Just what does that mean?" I ask Angel. I am re-thinking my portrait just now. I draw horns on the top of her head. I'm thinking of Rosemary's Baby, the movie, and how Mia Farrow had a devil baby. I wonder if Angel will have the devil's baby some day. "I bore a dead baby last year and no one saw but me," Angel says. I'm used to her mumblings now and I hear every word she says with precision. "I'm gonna have a baby this summer," I say to Angel. "I know," Angel says as she keeps a steady hand on the chalk.

The substitute teacher stands behind Angel and says," that's an interesting drawing." She holds Angel's portrait up and the class is quiet. For the first time I recognize the tear and it is clearly my own.

how you felt when I disappointed you

tony rauch

I had this friend who kept an old pen up on the top shelf of his locker. We used it to alter our report cards. The school district had budget problems, so all the report cards were printed in a hazy, faded blue which merely required a hazy, fading blue pen to award yourself with the grade you desired. He'd open up the envelope in homeroom and sigh and say, "Yep, looks like it's time to visit the pen."

One day my friend announced he was going out for the football team. He was fast and athletic. We had played basketball together for years. He used to talk like an announcer all the time, but not in a boastful way, more because he'd do these amazing things. He'd even do instant replays every now and then. "Let's see that again," he'd say as if proudly freezing a play in his head forever.

He was damn good; he could be a running back, or anything really. I was kind of jealous, you know, imagining him in that slow motion, scoring touchdowns and hanging out with all the football guys at that pitch dark pizza place after games on Friday nights. He'd have cheerleaders around him and get treated nicely by everyone. His life would be that of a celebrity, mysterious and unpredictable. Could you picture anyone being so lucky in all your life? Could you?

For a few days I was weighed down with those thoughts, my mind wet with photos of him in the newspapers and yearbook, dreaming it was me and not him. I'd bring him along to the pizza place and introduce him to all the cheerleaders, maybe even set him up. But gradually I knew that he would be him, and I would be me, and he would be introducing me to them. I wondered if he'd forget all about me, you know, like a mild cold.

I found out a week later that he couldn't go out for the team. I overheard some guy mentioning it really casually as I was settling down in the cafeteria. He had to work on the farm after school and couldn't get a ride back into town or something.

I sat there in the cafeteria as people came and went, getting up and sitting down with their books and lunch trays and back packs, coming and going, bitching about some teacher or some girl. I pictured him with those cheerleaders and those touchdowns and those popular people, experiencing those exotic places on Friday nights, being a part of something. He had a herd of friends, all of them pretty and self-assured. I saw him laughing and making out with that Michelle girl, real slowly in the leaves, like golden blankets under a tree in moonlight, the blankets rolling and twisting and glowing. I felt good for him there, proud as hell, sweating with pride for him, like he belonged there. And I was good there, too, cheering for him up in the stands on crisp, dark fall nights. So good that I felt terribly bad inside. A hazing, fading blue sky bad, like I was being crushed, like he had died years ago and I had just happened to remember him for that moment, that fading moment, picturing him with his touchdowns and with her under that tree at midnight – as if I were reading his mind.